Like The Wind

J L Williams

To William Codlin, jockey and animal whisper,
thank you for sharing your story.

Edited by Lisette de Jong
Published by Ocean Echo Books

ISBN 978-1-7385951-3-6

Praise for Like The Wind:

Like The Wind has it all: drama, heartache, pathos and fulfilment. I finished the previous book, Holding The Horse, eager to know what the future would hold for Sid, and here it is – a compelling sequel that weaves the threads of Sid's ongoing adventures to reach an incredible conclusion.

Patricia Fenton, author of 'Beyond the Rimu Grove' and 'War Bride'.

This was a very enjoyable read. It is well written and holds your attention and interest. From a (generalist) medical perspective I am happy that it represents the trauma issues sensitively and appropriately.

Dr A Walpole, Rural GP and RDA Volunteer

A wild ride from beginning to end!
F R M Riley, Author

Like The Wind deals with themes of trauma, especially as related to war, and the power of horses as healers.

Charitable Donation: Riding for the Disabled (RDA) caters to a diverse group of riders who benefit from sensory therapy riding lessons, run by dedicated volunteers and staff members. When the group first started there was a focus on physical disability, but with advancements in the medical field around identifying and treating other disabilities, many attendees are neurodiverse, or struggling with social anxiety. One dollar from the sale of every copy of this book will be donated to RDA New Zealand. To learn more about the RDA please visit their website: https://rda.org.nz

Contents

1. A change in the Weather — 1

2. Letters — 7

3. An Ultimatum — 11

4. Christchurch — 21

5. Ridgeway Racing Stables — 29

6. Not A Warm Welcome — 37

7. Lunchtime Shock — 43

8. Riding for Mr MacDonald — 49

9. Not Too Shabby — 53

10. Greaseball — 61

11. Horse Therapy — 69

12. A Tour of the Stables — 75

13. Home — 81

14. Auntie Glad — 87

15. Horses Are Healers — 97

16. A Dangerous Wind — 105

17. Caught Out — 109

18.	The Nor'wester	113
19.	Work	119
20.	Manawa	125
21.	Smoke	131
22.	Trouble	135
23.	Wade Daker	141
24.	The Perfect Team	147
25.	The Trials	151
26.	Sid's Race	157
27.	Vigilantes	165
28.	To The Rescue	169
29.	The Hobo	177
30.	Distraction	183
31.	The Well	187
32.	Spinning In Darkness	193
33.	Daniel Connolley	197
34.	Too Late	203
35.	Riccarton Racetrack	207
36.	Horse Whisperer	211
37.	The New Zealand Cup Race	213
38.	Sarah	219
39.	Winning and Losing	223
40.	Christchurch Square	227
Author's Note		231

Chapter One

A change in the Weather

Sid lay on his back in the shade of the Thorndon house, two precious envelopes clutched in his hand. Skylarks sang in the sky high above, and fine spring grass tickled the back of his neck. Just above his nose, a ladybird walked along the edge of a glossy, green hydrangea leaf.

Today was his sixteenth birthday; his first birthday since his family had moved to far away Christchurch. He was pretty sure nobody here knew it. And would they care, even if they knew?

He looked around. The garden was quiet apart from the soft stirring of the poplars. He was grateful for the broad-leaved hydrangea bushes hiding him from curious eyes. It was his favourite spot, hidden around the side of the house. A nice private spot where he could stop in a shady area and read his mail before trekking through the open paddock back to the stable.

It had been a day like any other at Thorndon Stables. Even now, the sound of men's voices and the whinny of a horse reached his ears from over at the track. The fragrance of turf roughened by racing hooves drifted on the wind. But the letters he held in his hand told him that at least two people in the world had remembered what day it was. He studied the envelopes. One was plain white, with his mother's clear, cursive handwriting looping across its surface. His throat tightened at the sight of it. He missed his mum and dad and his brothers and sisters. Rangiora was a long way from here.

The other letter, in a large pink envelope, was from Sarah Thorndon. Sarah, at boarding school in Wellington. He read his name and address, inscribed in her dainty, curling script, and imagined her hand, writing his name. Holding this envelope made his heart thump.

He held it up to the light. It seemed to contain a card. He sniffed it. Did it smell faintly of perfume? Actually, no, it didn't. That must be only in books, he thought, smiling at his own foolishness.

So, which to open first? He wanted to save Sarah's letter for later, but he found his fingers slipping under the top of the rosebud-pink envelope and tearing it open along the fold.

Suddenly, above him, voices sounded, floating out from an open window. He froze as the voices became louder, and he heard his own name. "Sid? Yes, he just came and got his letters." It was Mrs Thorndon's voice. "He had one from his family, and another one from Sarah. He looked very happy when I handed them to him."

Sid could hear the smile in Mrs Thorndon's voice. She had mothered him in her formal, English sort of way, since he'd been staying with them. He didn't live in the house, he slept in the bunk room with the other jockeys, but Sid always felt that she had a soft spot for him. Mr Thorndon's voice was gruff. "Does she still write to him?"

"Not as often," said Mrs Thorndon. "I think it's a card. It's his birthday today."

"Is it?" asked Mr Thorndon.

"Yes. His mother told me the date before they left." She laughed indulgently. "When Sarah first went away, she wrote to Sid every week. And drew hearts on the envelope! These days, the envelopes aren't decorated." She hesitated. "But this latest envelope is pale pink."

Mr Thorndon snorted. "We didn't bring her up to get involved with a stable boy."

"They're only writing letters, dear."

"Hearts! Pink envelopes! That girl needs to grow up. And she needs to raise her sights."

"I think it's sweet," said Mrs Thorndon.

Mr Thorndon's rumbling voice became louder. "Sid's a good boy, from a decent family, but he's no match for our Sarah. She's a cut above him, and he ought to know it and back off."

"Come on, Gerald, that's not fair. And he's not a stable boy, he's your most promising jockey." Mrs Thorndon's voice was sharp. "You said so yourself, he's very gifted. And of course they're friends. They were next-door neighbours for years."

"Friends!" spluttered Mr Thorndon. "When she draws hearts on the envelopes?"

Sid found that he'd been holding his breath, and let it out carefully. He felt his face burning. He sat up and glanced around, looking for a way of escape. Tight bunches of green and white hydrangea blossoms bobbed against his head, smelling like school erasers. In summer, they would swell into huge frilly balloons of blue and lilac. He didn't dare move, or the Thorndons might see him from the window. See him and think he was eavesdropping. Which he was, technically. But not intentionally. He'd have to sit tight now and wait until they went away. A sudden tickle in his throat created a strong urge to cough, and he swallowed hard to suppress it. He most certainly didn't want to be seen.

He inched further in under the cover of the hydrangeas as the voices fell silent. Over the fence, he could see several horses peacefully grazing. Should he try and sneak away to the paddock? But there was no chance the Thorndons wouldn't see him if he did.

The clink of glasses from the room above him made him feel thirsty, and he hoped they'd hurry up and go away so he could leave. Although, to be honest, it was a very interesting conversation they were having.

Mrs Thorndon spoke again. "You're proud of that boy, Gerald. He's got a special way with horses. You're always saying that."

"He's a good jockey," said Mr Thorndon grudgingly. "He's been winning his races."

"Lara Wilson asked if he could help with their filly," said Mrs Thorndon.

"All the horse owners are asking for his help," admitted Mr Thorndon. "He knows how to get the best out of a horse. He can calm them down like a charm."

"It's like magic," said Mrs Thorndon. "It's wonderful to see."

"He understands horses," said Mr Thorndon. "He's almost as good as my father." He paused. "Where's *our* letter from Sarah? Has she written to her own family?"

"Of course she has," said Mrs Thorndon. "Just a short letter. And she'll be home in a couple of months, for the holidays."

"Yes." Mr Thorndon's voice sounded grim.

Sid could imagine his frown; the broad, usually kindly English face, with its dark brows drawn together. A good man, but Sid was always a bit afraid of him. Not without reason. His night-riding escapade on the beach last year had ended in disaster. Only Sid's bravery when Sarah's grandfather was looking down the barrel of a gun had changed Mr Thorndon from a furious neighbour to a supportive employer.

Mr Thorndon's voice became louder, sounding like he was right above where Sid was hiding. "When is Sarah due back, exactly?" he asked.

He must be at the window, Sid thought. He ducked his head down, making sure the bushes hid him.

"A week before Christmas," Mrs Thorndon answered.

"Two months," said Mr Thorndon softly.

"I suppose that's not so long," said Mrs Thorndon, "but I'm counting the days. I can't wait to see her. The days sometimes seem so long and empty without our Sarah."

"I'll be in my office, Jane. I need to make a phone call."

"Who are you telephoning? You haven't finished your drink."

"I'll take it with me," Mr Thorndon replied. "I'm phoning a chap I know. Name of Ridgeway. Act now, that's the ticket."

"Ridgeway," said Mrs Thorndon. "That name's familiar."

"You've met him. John Ridgeway. He owns Ridgeway Racing Stables, near Riccarton Racetrack in Christchurch. He owes me a favour. I heard his top jockey had an accident and can't ride. I think he needs a new jockey. And I need one less."

"Oh, Gerald!" protested Mrs Thorndon. "You're doing a marvellous job training Sid. He's going to make you very proud. Don't you want to see that? The boy's achieving his dream."

"He can do that at Ridgeways," said Mr Thorndon.

"Shifting him to somewhere else could set him back," Mrs Thorndon said.

"Set him back? Not him," said Mr Thorndon. "He's like a ferret after a rabbit, that boy. Nothing will stop him, short of another war. Ridgeway's will be good for him. It'll help his career along. Biggest track he could race on, down there. It's the place to be if you want to make a name for yourself, which he does."

Sid was stunned.

A ferret after a rabbit. That's offensive.

He tuned his ears back in to the conversation.Mrs Thorndon was saying, "Honestly, He'll make you proud, Gerald. He'll make Thorndon stables proud."

"He's a fine jockey," said Mr Thorndon, "but he's not suitable for our Sarah. She's got her future to think of. She needs to keep her mind on her studies. I'm not risking it, Jane. I'm packing him off so he won't be around when she comes home. I don't want her to be distracted at this very important time in her life."

"You're interfering," said Mrs Thorndon. "Interfering in young people's lives. And what will Sarah say?

"Two months," said Mr Thorndon. "Plenty of time. I'm off to make that phone call. I'll be in my office, Jane."

Sid heard his heavy footsteps leaving the room.

Mrs Thorndon called after him, "At least he'll be near his family. But I don't know if you're doing the right thing."

Sid almost gasped aloud.

Did that mean what he thought it meant? Mr Thorndon was shipping him out. Getting rid of him. For something he hadn't even done.

His heart thumping, he watched the ladybird reach the very tip of the leaf. A ladybird; living its brief life, unaware of the humans and their dramas. The warm smell of damp earth and growing things filled his nostrils, but it didn't calm him. Before his eyes, the ladybird spread its wings and flew away.

Sarah, thought Sid. They're getting rid of me because of Sarah. Before she comes home.

He remembered his mother's words: "Eavesdroppers never hear anything good about themselves." It was true.

Chapter Two

Letters

When he was sure that the Thorndons were no longer in their living room, Sid scrambled to his feet. His breathing was loud in his ears as he stumbled out of their garden and across to the stables. He glanced back over his shoulder as he went, but no faces peered from the windows, and no one followed him.

The jockeys slept in a small building attached to the stallion yard. Sid slowed as he approached, listening for voices before opening the door. All was quiet, so he stepped inside. The overheard conversation still rang in his ears.

They were getting rid of him. His head spun. He blinked at the letters, and the desire to read them sprang up afresh.

Worry later, he told himself.

He climbed up to the top bunk where he slept and opened the window to let in some air. Dust motes danced in the breeze that drifted into the room, bringing with it the distant tang of the sea. It was one of those hot, peaceful days when it feels like summer is just around the corner.

The beach would be nice, he thought, then changed his mind. It wasn't a place he liked to go to any more. He never rode along the lane to the sea without a shiver of guilt, even though he'd sort of managed to get over his midnight beach disaster. The memory of that dark night with Mr Thorndon's injured horse hadn't stopped haunting him.

Silver still trusts me, though, Sid thought. Horses never ceased to amaze him, the way they trusted.

"They don't trust just anybody," his dad had said. "Horses know. They trust you because you're you. And that means a lot."

Those words meant a lot to Sid, too. He set aside the half-opened envelope from Sarah, tore open the envelope from his mother, and started reading.

Dear Sid

This is a quick note to wish you a very happy birthday and to let you know we are all well. We are all missing you, but we know you are in good hands with the Thorndons. Ruby is making great progress at Sumner School. Beryl visits her whenever she can take time off from her teacher training studies.

The twins are settling in at their new school and are turning into South Island kids just like I used to be. There's a craze for marbles at their school in Rangiora, just like there was in Foxton when you were at school. Can I let them have your old marbles? I told them they can't take them. They have to wait and see what you say, because you might want to hang on to them.

Dad sends his love and says hurry up and win another race so he can put the newspaper cutting up on the wall.

I'd better go now. I'm making ice cream today. Our neighbour along the road has an icebox in her fridge, and she lets me put the ice cream in there. I send the twins along with it. She even takes it out halfway through and beats it so it comes out nice and fluffy. She's a good neighbour.

Must run. Many happy returns.

Write soon

Mum xxxx

Sid set down the letter. He could picture his mother; busy in her kitchen, brushing her hair back from her forehead. She had flyaway hair that always escaped, no matter what she did. He smiled. Then, with a quickening heartbeat, he opened the letter from Sarah. It contained a card, with a picture of two horses grazing in an unnaturally green field with a rainbow above them in the sky. He opened it and a letter slipped out.

First, he read the card, smiling at the sight of her handwriting.

To Sid, wishing you a very happy birthday, love from Sarah.

Okay. Short and sweet. He unfolded the letter.

Dear Sid

Happy birthday! I hope this reaches you in time. How are you? School is good, and my friend Bridie and I had permission to go to her house last weekend. They have a swimming pool, but it's still too cold to swim. She lives in Kelburn, which is in Wellington. We have a new art teacher. She trained in Paris, so we are very lucky. Exams are coming up soon, so I must study hard and I don't have much time for writing letters.

I hope your training with Dad is going well.

Love from Sarah

Sid blinked.

What? Such a short letter. And it didn't say much.

He read it a second time, glanced back at the card, then perused the letter again. He frowned. He could tell she had written it in a hurry. It was almost a duty letter. He read it again, longing for more.

Don't be stupid. She's busy. Sid slid down from his bunk and paced the floor. She's got exams coming up. Of course, she doesn't have much time to write.

The bunk room darkened as a bulky figure filled the doorway, blocking out the brilliance of the sunlit yard outside. Mr Thorndon stood there, seeming even larger than usual.

"Sidney? I've got something to tell you. Come over to the house, can you? I'll be in my study."

"Yes, sir," said Sid.

"Had some letters?" Mr Thorndon asked.

Sid couldn't see Mr Thorndon's face because the light was behind him, but he knew his eyes would be taking in the pink envelope.

"Um, yes," he said. "From Mum. And, um, one from Sarah."

"So I hear." Mr Thorndon's voice sounded grumpy.

"I'll be over in a minute," said Sid.

"Thank you, Sidney." Mr Thorndon turned on his heel and marched away, the bright afternoon sun filling the doorway where he'd stood.

Chapter Three

An Ultimatum

Outside the bunk room, the golden light of the late afternoon sun slanted through the trees. In the east, gigantic towers of cumulus cloud had formed, glowing brilliant white in the sun, but followed by ominous columns of black. Birds swooped to the shelter of the garden, their clear calls signalling the end of the day. Sid could smell rain on the cool breeze that had sprung up.

Rain meant wet horses. The smell of a wet horse wasn't nearly as nice as the smell of a dry horse. Sid felt a sudden longing to visit his old horse Hugh, grazing in a nearby paddock, to throw his arms around his neck and soak up his horsey comfort. But he had to go and see Mr Thorndon.

He trudged over to the house, raised his fist, and knocked on the door.

"Hello, Sidney." Mr Thorndon opened the door.

He must have been standing right there, Sid realised. Waiting.

Mr Thorndon's gaze went directly to Sid's empty hands. "All right?" he asked.

"Yes," said Sid.

"Come in, come in." Mr Thorndon sounded falsely cheery.

Was he nervous? Sid wondered. Surely not. He held all the cards in this game, after all. But he didn't seem quite his usual self.

"Very nice that you had a letter from your family. We don't want our boys getting homesick, do we?" Mr Thorndon hesitated. "Come into the lounge, Sidney. I've got a proposition for you."

Sid followed reluctantly into the wide hallway of the villa. He had seldom been inside the Thorndons' home. The first time was that night Silver was injured on the beach. Since then, he'd been inside the house just a few times; to drink lemonade with Sarah, or to pick up his letters. But the terror of that midnight horse riding accident had stuck with him. The shame and fear of waking them in the middle of the night coloured his every visit to the Thorndon homestead. That night was seared into his memory for life.

"In here." Mr Thorndon led the way.

***

The lounge was golden in the evening light. The net curtains at the open windows stirred gently in the breeze, and Sid could smell the warm, cut-grass-and-flower fragrance of the garden. He could hear the faint rustle of the hydrangea bushes outside, where he'd recently hidden, eavesdropping. A clock ticked solemnly on the mantelpiece. A fat, plush sofa and two armchairs dominated the room, their curved arms bulging. In the centre of the room there was a small oak table, the carved patterns on its polished legs gleaming. An upright piano stood against the wall.

Mr Thorndon stopped by the small table. Sid stopped too and stood waiting.

Mr Thorndon said, "I'll come straight to the point. An opportunity has come up for you to move to Christchurch. I've just been talking to a friend of mine in the South Island, Mr John Ridgeway. He has a big racing stable near Riccarton Racetrack. They have a place for another jockey, and you have a chance to take that place."

Sid tried to look surprised. "Oh," he said.

"It's a top stable," said Mr Thorndon. "Ridgeways will give you all the opportunities you could ever want. They can do far more for you than I could." Mr Thorndon waved a hand towards the sofa. "Have a seat."

Sid sat carefully on the sofa. The fabric felt prickly to his touch. Not as soft as it appeared.

"Christchurch," he muttered. Conflicting emotions churned inside him. Indignation fought with a longing to see his family. He held himself in check. "I'm quite happy here, Mr Thorndon."

"That's good to hear, Sidney. But you're ambitious, aren't you?"

"Yes," Sid admitted.

"You want to be riding winners, winning big races?"

"Yes," said Sid again. This was true. It was what he'd always wanted, ever since he was a little boy.

"The thing is, Sidney, although you're doing well here, very well, you could do better. Foxton is tiny. Ridgeway's is a big racing stable in a major city. And John Ridgeway needs another jockey. I'll tell you what the situation is – his best rider just broke a leg."

Sid scowled.

Getting rid of me. Trying to make it sound like a great opportunity, he thought.

Mr Thorndon continued. "It wasn't a riding accident. The man broke his leg rock climbing. He's an older jockey, an exceptional rider. His name's Wade Daker. He has a great rapport with the stable's top horse, Manawa, and that's a horse very few people can even get close to. Daker was supposed to be riding him in the New Zealand Cup race, which, as you know, isn't far off. So now they've got a problem."

Sid said nothing.

"Anyhow," Mr Thorndon continued, "Daker's out of the running now, for the rest of the season at the very least. And Ridgeways is short of options. They need an expert rider who can get a good rapport with a difficult horse, and they need one now. I've been telling John about your unique talents."

Yeah, but he didn't ring you. You rang him. Sid didn't dare speak the words aloud.

"It's nothing," muttered Sid.

"It's not nothing," said Mr Thorndon. "You've got something very special. Everyone around here knows it." He gave Sid a hard look. "I thought you'd want to be close to your family."

That's a low blow, Sid thought. At one time, he would have leaped at the chance, if only he hadn't overheard that recent conversation.

"So you're sending me to Christchurch?" he asked, his heart rate increasing as his sense of outrage grew.

"As long as you're in agreement," said Mr Thorndon. "It's all arranged. All you need to do is grab the opportunity. Think about it, Sidney. It's the best possible thing for you. You'll be near your family. You'll be keeping up with your apprenticeship, and you'll be working with a horse tipped to win the Cup. What do you think about that?"

"What do I think?" Sid's heart was thumping so fast he could hardly breathe. "Why do they want me?" he blurted out.

Mr Thorndon raised an eyebrow. "I just told you," he said.

Sid tried again. "I mean, why do they want me, and not one of the local blokes? They're probably all more experienced than I am."

"John needs someone pretty special to ride Manawa. As I said, I've told him what an excellent rider you are," said Mr Thorndon. "And that you've got a unique way with horses. Quite remarkable." Mr

Thorndon cleared his throat. His tone of voice hardened. "You might never get another chance like this."

Did those words hide a veiled threat? Mr Thorndon's face looked so fierce Sid turned his eyes away. He looked out of the window at the fading daylight.

"You'd be near your family. You'd like that, wouldn't you?" said Mr Thorndon, sounding suddenly falsely jolly.

"Yes," said Sid.

"And you want to be a top jockey, don't you?"

"Yes," said Sid miserably. He allowed his gaze to wander around the room, examining the ornaments and photographs. There was a framed picture of Sarah on top of the piano.

"You'd miss Sarah, of course," acknowledged Mr Thorndon, following his gaze.

Sid felt his cheeks burn. Mr Thorndon had never actually said anything to him before about Sarah. "Yes," he said. "And she'll be home soon, for the holidays, and I wouldn't be here."

"No, you wouldn't," agreed Mr Thorndon.

Did Sid imagine it, or was there a ring of satisfaction to those words?

Mr Thorndon cleared his throat. "I'm going down to Christchurch myself in November, for the Cup race." He eyed Sid. "Sarah will accompany me. I've arranged with her school for her to have a couple of days away."

"Oh." Sid's heart lifted. Maybe Mr Thorndon wasn't so totally against him, after all. "Really?"

"Yes. I arranged our trip some time ago and I won't be changing anything. The train and ferry tickets are all booked. She'd be disappointed if she didn't go. The Ridgeways are old friends."

Not for my sake then, Sid thought. "Oh, I see," he said. He hesitated, remembering something. "What about my wages? Do I get my wages if I'm leaving?"

"I'll have your wages transferred to Ridgeway's. He'll continue the apprenticeship for you and you'll get paid out at the end of your five years, just like you would have if you'd stayed here," said Mr Thorndon.

"Oh," said Sid, the sudden vision of lots of money vanishing away. He remembered something else. "I was going to write to my mum. What shall I tell her?"

"You want to go?" Mr Ridgeway asked.

"I don't have much choice," said Sid, failing to keep the bitterness out of his voice.

"Of course you have a choice, boy," Mr Thorndon growled. His already loud voice grew louder. "You can stay here if you want to."

Sid knew instantly how impossible that would be. How awkward. How every day would be miserable, knowing he wasn't wanted.

Mr Thorndon continued, "But you'd regret it. It's a golden opportunity. You'd be a fool to turn it down. Chances like this don't come along every day."

"No," said Sid. He knew he was doomed. He couldn't fight it. But he'd be fighting inside, all the way to Christchurch.

Mr Thorndon stared at him, unblinking.

Sid felt himself shrink under that gaze. "You could be right," he muttered.

Mr Thorndon smiled. "You won't regret it," he said.

Sid wasn't so sure about that, but he couldn't argue. "Can I have the address of the stables? So I can tell Mum?"

"Of course. Here, let me get you a piece of paper and you can write it down."

Mr Thorndon laid a sheet of paper on the small oak table that stood between them and handed Sid a fountain pen. It was heavy. A quality pen. Everything here was quality. Mr Thorndon dictated the new address.

Ridgeway Stables

Racecourse Road

Riccarton

Christchurch

Sid wrote carefully, aware of Mr Thorndon's eyes watching him. He tried to make the letters even, but his hand shook and the words juddered across the surface of the paper.

How things can change in a moment. Just like that.

He replaced the cap on the pen and handed it back. "Thanks, Mr Thorndon."

"Not at all, Sidney. I know you're itching for a big race. Now's your chance. I'll telephone Ridgeway to confirm it, and it's a done deal."

Sudden anxiety clutched at Sid's heart. "What about Hugh?" he burst out.

Mr Thorndon's face softened. "Don't you worry about Hugh," he said. "He'll be happy here, enjoying his retirement years. I'm looking after Sarah's horse; I can look after yours as well. They'll keep each other company. Don't you worry about Hugh, Sidney. He'll always have a home here."

"Thanks, Mr Thorndon."

"Not at all, Sidney," said Mr Thorndon. "So, it's all settled. I'm booking you a ticket on the train to Wellington, and on the ferry to Lyttelton. Then you'll be met by a friend of mine and put on a train to Christchurch. I'll write to your father, and he can meet you off the train when you get there."

Sid stared at Mr Thorndon. He had it all planned. Every detail.

His head spun with crazy thoughts.

I won't go. I'll run away. But even as he thought it, he knew it was a dumb idea.

But they couldn't stop him from writing to Sarah. And they wouldn't be able to stop her writing back to him. Mr Thorndon believed his daughter was too good for him. He'd prove him wrong. And he'd see her again. November was only a month away.

"Off you go, then," said Mr Thorndon. "Better get your belongings sorted out. You'll be off before you know it."

As Sid reached the door of the living room, Mr Thorndon called him back.

"Sidney, I've just remembered; I've got something for you." He fished in his pocket. "It's not brand new, but it's rather nice." He held out a pocket knife with a polished wooden handle. "My wife told me it's your birthday today. I've had this since I was a boy. Very attached to it, I was, all my life. I brought it out here from England when we came over, but I haven't used it for quite a long time." He looked down at the knife, a wry smile on his face. "I always intended to give it to Sarah, but she's not the sort of girl who likes knives. She never was a tomboy, our Sarah. Too much of a lady." He held out the knife. "I'd like you to have it, Sidney."

Sid took the knife. It felt good in his hand. Just the right weight, the handle smooth to his touch. He dug his thumbnail into the groove in the blade and prised it out.

"It's good and sharp," said Mr Thorndon. "I sharpened it myself, just now." Mr Thorndon's eyes were hard to read. "I've always liked that knife. I think you're just the person to be its new owner."

Sid brushed his thumb tentatively across the blade. He could tell it was beautifully sharp.

"Sheffield steel," said Mr Thorndon. "It won't let you down."

"Thanks, Mr Thorndon," said Sid, suddenly moved. This man had been very good to him. He'd given him a chance, even when he'd almost killed his favourite horse on that crazy midnight ride on the beach. He respected Mr Thorndon. But he resented being sent away because of Sarah. His frustration burned hot inside him. A pocket knife was no substitute for a girlfriend. He closed the knife and slipped it into his pocket.

"Thank you," he said. He couldn't make his face smile. There was another knife twisting inside him that hurt too much.

"You're a good boy, Sidney," said Mr Thorndon. "You'll go far, if you keep on the way you're going." He held out his hand. "All the best for the future, lad."

Sid shook the broad hand and looked up into the man's eyes. Did he read regret there? Or satisfaction? Mr Thorndon was getting rid of him, yes. But in a kindly way, and with respect. Sid felt strangely honoured, even though indignation still burned in his heart. As he let go of Mr Thorndon's hand, he sensed a significant moment, a transition. It was one of those moments in time where you know that nothing after it will ever be the same again.

"Thank you, Mr Thorndon," he said.

He turned and hurried out of the room, suddenly desperate to get away.

Life moves in chunks, he thought. It clunks around, like the hands of a clock. It pretends to flow like a river, but suddenly, there's a big change. Suddenly, it's a different season, almost overnight. That's how life works.

Outside the house, Sid looked up at the sky. It was full of thick black clouds now, rolling masses of unshed vapour, blocking the sun and shadowing the garden. An early darkness leaped out from the shrubby borders like the foreboding that swamped his heart. Seeing Mum and

Dad – that would be wonderful. Losing the hope of a summer with Sarah – that filled his heart with gloom.

Chapter Four

Christchurch

S id disembarked at Lyttelton, clutching his leather suitcase, and was carried along with the crowd of passengers down the gangplank and onto the wharf. Seagulls screamed overhead, and the wind pushed him sideways and whipped his hair around as he struggled to find his feet again on dry land. A hand grabbed his shoulder.

"Sidney Everett?" It was a tall, kindly looking man in a thick coat and brown felt hat.

"Yes," answered Sid.

"Cecil Gardener. I'm a friend of Gerald Thorndon's. He asked me to meet you." He held out his hand and Sid shook it. "This way. You just need to follow the crowd, really, but Gerald wanted to make sure you got there safely."

I'll bet he did, thought Sid.

"Thank you," he said politely.

The electrified locomotive waited at the station, with passenger coaches behind.

"Oh," said Sid. "Not a steam engine?"

"No," said the man. "Very advanced. All electrified in Christchurch, too." He looked at Sid. "Are you all right?" he asked.

"Yes," said Sid.

"On you hop, then," said the man. "Your father will meet you at the other end. All the best."

Sid found a seat next to the window. The man waved from the platform, then turned on his heel and walked away.

***

The train racketed through a tunnel carved through rock.

"No nasty smoke," said a lady sitting opposite Sid, as they plunged out of the tunnel into daylight. Her two children stared at him, not speaking.

Sid stretched his travel-stiffened legs. Around him, fellow travellers were gathering their bags and coats, preparing to alight at the station not far ahead. Sid pulled his coat on and picked up his suitcase.

"Got someone meeting you, dear?" asked the woman.

"Yes, my family," said Sid.

"Oh, that's good. On a visit, are you?" she asked.

"I'm here to work. At Ridgeways," said Sid.

"Oh, I know," she said. "The big stables." She smiled at him. "Jockey, are you?"

"Yes."

"You look like one. Well, good luck."

"Thank you," said Sid.

The train slowed, sliding into the shadow of Christchurch railway station. The building soared above, its tall, swooping arches just like a cathedral's.

Sid scanned the milling crowd on the platform, searching for the faces of his family, especially the longed-for, familiar face of his mother. He smiled an anticipatory smile of pure joy at seeing them all again. He had to keep reminding himself that his family didn't know Mr

Thorndon had sent him down here just to get rid of him. They would think it was a wonderful thing. They'd be really excited.

The train slid to a halt, coming to rest with a final shudder. A whistle blew, and the doors opened, letting in the chill Christchurch air with its whiff of industry. Sid could sense the bustle and hum of a teeming city. Everyone in the coach surged towards the door. He joined the exiting crowd.

A movie poster on a wall caught his attention: "David Copper-field." A Charles Dickens novel his teacher had read to his class. It seemed a long time ago, even though it had only been last year. He felt, for a moment, a surge of nostalgia for his small country school, and Mr Cowley, his teacher.

There was a thump on his shoulder.

"Sid!" His sister Beryl pounced on him, hugging him, then punching him on the arm, just like she always used to do. "You're as skinny as ever!" she said.

She was a year older and appeared every bit the school teacher she was training to be. Her cardigan, surely knitted by Mum, had small pearly buttons that gleamed in the sunlight.

"Excuse me, Miss," he said. "I'm looking for the Everett family."

She laughed, punching him again. "Here they come," she said.

The Everetts surrounded him. His younger brothers Bill and Bruce were grinning up at him. Mum and Dad looked happier than he'd seen them in years. He glanced around for Ruby.

Mum understood who he was looking for. "Ruby's at school," she said. "They wouldn't give her the day off. But fair enough. Those deaf children have to work harder than anyone else just to keep up." She put a hand on Sid's shoulder and held him at arm's length. "You're looking well, Sidney. Growing up." She smiled. "Are you excited to be here?"

"Yup," he said. And it was true. His indignation at being chucked out by Mr Thorndon still burned, but he was overjoyed to see his family again.

One of his brothers tugged at his arm. "We've got ferrets," said Bill.

"Ferrets?" said Sid.

"Yeah, for rabbiting. You send a ferret down the rabbit hole and it flushes all the rabbits out. Then we catch them."

"We get paid a lot of money for the skins," said Bruce. "We catch loads of rabbits. They're everywhere."

"You should see them, Sid," said Bill. "The rabbits. There are thousands of them."

"You have to see our ferrets," said Bruce. "Mine is called Foxy, and Bill's is called Finch."

"Because we've got a teacher at school called Mr Finch and he looks just like a ferret," said Bill.

Sid nodded. He'd heard of the South Island rabbit problem. "That'd be interesting, boys," he said. "I'd love to see your ferrets." He looked around at his dad.

There he was. Dad. Tall and lean, but broad-shouldered. His bony face was glowing with pleasure. "Hello, Sid." he said.

Sid felt an enormous wave of happiness well up inside him. He hadn't realised how much he'd missed his dad. The same father who had seemed like his worst enemy a year ago was now his biggest racing fan.

Dad was smiling, holding out his hand. Sid shook it, feeling strange. He'd rarely shaken hands with his father before. Maybe once in his whole life. It seemed like Dad was treating him like he was grown up now.

"Good to see you, son." Dad smiled his rare, crooked smile. "How are you doing?"

"All right, Dad," said Sid. He might have said more, but his emotions suddenly swamped his heart.

"You've grown, son," said Dad. "Looking like a man." He too, held Sid at a distance, surveying him. "Mr Thorndon must think a lot of you, eh? Sending you to a big operation like Ridgeways."

Sid gulped. He wasn't being sent to Ridgeways because Mr Thorndon 'thought a lot of him.' He didn't reply.

"Winning races?" asked Dad.

"Yup," said Sid. "I've saved a few newspaper cuttings."

Dad's smile was even bigger, making his face look years younger. "Got a spare one for me to pin up on my wall?"

Sid laughed. "They're for you, Dad. If you want them."

"Of course I do," said Dad. He put an arm around Sid, pulling him into his shoulder.

"They're in my bag," said Sid. "I'll give them to you when we get home."

"I'm taking you straight to Ridgeways, son," said Dad. "It's not far from here. It's quite a long way out to our place. I'll come and get you once you've settled in, and bring you home for a visit."

"Oh. Okay," said Sid. He hadn't expected that. Now that he saw his family, all he wanted was to go home and be with them.

"Mr Ridgeway wants you there straight away, apparently," said Mum. "It's what we were told. Mr Thorndon organised it."

"I'll bet he did," said Sid grimly.

Mum stared at him in surprise, but he didn't explain. He couldn't bear to tell his family the truth. Better to let them think it was some sort of promotion.

"It's a great opportunity for you, Sid," said Mum.

"Yes," said Sid. He needed to change the subject. "I've missed you."

Mum scooped him up into a tight hug that felt like coming home. "We've missed you too, Sidney. More than you know." After a moment, she stepped back and straightened her hat.

"Is that a new hat, Mum?" asked Sid.

"Yes," she smiled. "I needed something smarter, for Christchurch. Wait until you see it, Sid. Very grand."

Dad took Sid's bag from him. "Pity you have to go straight there," he said. "I wanted to show you the farm. And we could use your help. The twins need to grow a bit before they're much use."

"Awww, Dad!" protested Bill. "We're nearly eleven years old."

"And they're more interested in catching rabbits than anything else," said Dad.

"Yeah, because we make money from the skins," said Bruce. "Although they're changing how much you get paid. I think it's going to be less, soon."

Dad ruffled Bruce's hair. "You're not doing too bad, son," he smiled. "All right, everyone, let's get Sid to the stables. He's got a race to win."

Beryl pointed to the film poster for David Copperfield.

"We went to see that," she said. "The film isn't the same as the book. They missed out that whole bit where he goes to the horrible boarding school."

"I don't remember him going to boarding school," said Sid.

"Yes, you do. You know – the bit where they hang a sign around his neck that says 'He Bites.'"

"Oh, yeah, I remember. I suppose they can't fit everything into a film," said Sid vaguely. "Tell me a bit more about Ruby," he asked. "How's she going at Sumner? Does she like it?"

"Yes, she likes it," said Beryl. "And she's made some friends."

Mum said, "Poor little things. But they seem happy enough."

Beryl laughed. "Mum, Ruby loves it there."

"Best thing for her," said Dad. "Learning to talk, she is."

"Really?" said Sid.

"Yes," said Dad, "and it sounds like proper words. Wait till you hear her." Dad picked up Sid's suitcase. "Come on, Sid, we'll find the car. Got a car now. Morris Oxford. Fits us all in." He strode off.

Sid followed. A newspaper headline on a board outside a tobacconist's kiosk caught his eye.

Missing Ex-soldier

Police fear for the safety of returned serviceman Daniel Connolley, missing from his home in North East Valley, Dunedin. Connolley served in the army in the Pacific War, where he was captured by Japanese forces. He managed to escape, along with one of his fellow soldiers. Once recovered, he was able to return to duty and remained on active service until the end of the conflict. There are concerns for his mental condition. Anyone with information regarding the whereabouts of Sergeant Daniel Connolley is requested to contact the nearest police station immediately.

"Hurry up, Sid," shouted his brothers.

Sid hurried.

Chapter Five

Ridgeway Racing Stables

Crammed in the back seat of the car between his brothers and Beryl, Sid leaned back, letting the family's chatter wash over him. The comfort of hearing their voices was as soothing as lying in a deep, hot bath. He closed his eyes, allowing his weary muscles to relax.

Mum's voice rose above the rest. "I wish we could take you home, Sid," she said.

Sid opened his eyes. "Yeah," he said.

She had turned around to look at him from the front seat of the car. "But you'll see our place when you get some time off." Her expression was wistful. Then she brightened. "But I bet you're excited! I wonder what this Ridgeways place is like?"

Ridgeways. Sid's heart lurched as he turned the word over in his mind.

"Yeah," said Sid again. "I wonder too."

There would be jockeys, of course. More than at the Thorndon's. He already knew that. Jockeys, trainers, stable-hands, even a proper kitchen with kitchen staff, and a big training track. Mr Thorndon had described it to him. A first-class training facility, he'd called it. Somehow, Sid wasn't sure if he wanted first class any more. He already missed Thorndon Stables. He missed the earthy smell of the surrounding farmland and the distant salt tang of the sea when the wind blew from the coast.

"Not far," said Dad. "We'll soon be there."

Sid looked out of the window. They had left the city centre behind and were now in some sort of industrial area. They passed some enormous buildings with lots of bicycles parked outside, and one or two big old sheds that seemed derelict and falling into decay. There was a gloomy stand of big old kahikatea trees. Then they left all that behind, and the wide, green world of the racetrack opened out before them.

Sid stared as they drove in through the imposing gates of Ridgeway Racing Stables. It was bigger and grander than he had imagined. Wooden post and rail fences ran on either side of the driveway. Horses grazed in nearby paddocks. Ahead was a cluster of buildings, with one standing out larger than all the rest.

His father stopped the car in front of this larger building and turned off the engine. In the stillness, Sid could hear birds chirping. Tall trees, glowing with the fresh green of springtime, stood dotted about the neatly trimmed lawn, their leaves gently stirring in the breeze. Newly planted flower beds flanked a path to the main entrance. Several bicycles were parked around the side of the building, and a gleaming Bedford truck stood in the driveway, with 'Ridgeway Stables' sign-written on the side.

"Very nice," said Mum.

"Here we are," said Dad. "Come along, Sidney."

Sid climbed out after Beryl, stretching his tired legs. The air smelled of flowers and freshly cut grass, reminding him of Mrs Thorndon's garden. The fine gravel of the car park crunched under his boots. He felt dizzy from travelling for so long, but his worries faded away, just a little. This place looked very professional. A stable he could be proud to work for. Excitement bubbled up inside him.

Dad opened the boot of the car and pulled out Sid's small leather suitcase. He banged the boot shut again and patted the shiny black vehicle. "Not new, but she goes great," he said.

Sid smiled. The car was a surprise. The family had never had a car before. It seemed so strange to see his family in a different world, and owning a car.

Dad raised an eyebrow. "You ready, son?" he asked.

"Yup," said Sid. "As ready as I'll ever be."

***

Sid walked with his father into the imposing building. Mum followed behind with Beryl and the twins.

Inside was a spacious entrance foyer. Behind the counter, a lady sat typing at a desk. On the counter there was a bell and a vase of spring flowers.

Mum buried her nose in the flowers and inhaled deeply. "Mmmmm. Freesias."

The lady looked up and smiled. "Sweetest flower in the world," she said.

Beryl gazed around. "A lot fancier than the Thorndon's," she whispered to Sid.

Sid looked at the twins and grimaced. As usual, they looked scruffy. Bruce's hair stuck up on end. Bill's jumper had egg or something on the front. Mum spotted it at the same time as Sid. "Come here, Bill," she hissed. As soon as he was near enough, she whipped off his jumper and stuffed it into her handbag.

"Mum!" protested Bill.

"Grubby," said Mum shortly. "Shush."

The lady got up from her typewriter and came to the counter. "Can I help you?" she asked.

"We're here to see Mr Ridgeway," said Dad. "This is my son Sidney, come down from Foxton. Mr Ridgeway's expecting us."

"Oh, yes." The lady smiled down at Sid. "Hang on a minute, dear, I'll get him." She looked at Dad. "It's Mr Everett, isn't it?"

"Yes," said Dad.

The family stood awkwardly as the lady went away, her heels tapping on the polished wooden floor.

"It's a big place," said Mum.

Nobody else said anything. Sid bit his lip, excitement churning inside him.

A door opened, and a bulky, grey-suited figure approached. "Good morning, good morning!" he roared.

Mr Ridgeway had round, red cheeks and a beaming face. Sid noticed that his suit buttons were straining at the buttonholes.

"Here you are, eh?" shouted Mr Ridgeway. "The golden boy from Thorndon's." He turned to Sid's dad. "John Ridgeway," he said heartily, holding out his hand.

"Arthur Everett," said Dad, shaking Mr Ridgeway's hand.

Sid gulped. He eyed Mr Ridgeway warily, but the man seemed genuinely enthusiastic. He watched as Mr Ridgeway shook hands with his dad and nodded respectfully to his mum.

"And how's my old mate, Gerald?" Mr Ridgeway asked Sid.

"Mr Thorndon? He's alright," said Sid. What else could he say? "He's in very good health," he added.

Mr Ridgeway roared with laughter. "Very good health, eh? Well, I'm pleased to hear it. And how's that lovely daughter of his?"

Sid felt his face flushing. "She's at boarding school in Wellington."

"So I hear," said Mr Ridgeway. "Growing up, like all young people." He glanced at the twins, and his face became a little less cheerful. "Shall we go into the office?"

"I'll take the twins outside," offered Mum. "Come on, boys. Let the men do their talking." She shepherded them back out into the sunshine. Beryl gave Sid a quick, encouraging smile, then she followed her mother and the twins outside.

***

Mr Ridgeway's office was like a hall of fame. There was a strong smell of leather and silver polish, and trophies covered the shelves. The photographs on the walls were all of horses and their riders.

The men sat, and Sid stood.

Mr Ridgeway picked up a piece of paper from his desk. "Your son has an outstanding commendation from Gerald Thorndon," he said to Sid's father. "Absolutely glowing. And as you probably know, we needed another jockey rather urgently. We're coming up to the New Zealand Cup, and there's a whole swag of other races going on at the same time. And our most experienced jockey went and broke his leg."

"Yes, I heard," said Dad. He hesitated. "I assumed Mr Daker had a riding accident, but apparently he was rock climbing."

"We haven't had a riding accident for a while, touch wood." Mr Ridgeway touched his fingers to his polished wooden desk. "Just the usual things boys get up to, that end in tears. Climbing trees. Daring each other to go into the industrial area. You would have passed through it. There are some old, derelict buildings there. It's out of bounds." He shot a stern look at Sid.

Sid nodded automatically. He wasn't interested in old, industrial buildings.

Mr Ridgeway continued, "Yes, Daker had a climbing accident. He's an experienced climber, but he had a fall, and that was that. You've probably heard of him. Wade Daker is one of the top jockeys in New Zealand. He has an amazing way with horses, and with Manawa in particular."

"Manawa," said Dad. "That's a famous name."

"Yes," said Mr Ridgeway. "Our top horse. Lots of wins. But he's a horse that needs a special person to handle him. And he's even more grumpy and difficult now that Wade isn't here." He looked at Sid. "Sidney?"

Sid jumped. "Yes, sir?"

"Welcome aboard. I'll introduce you to everyone this evening. In the meantime, I'll get one of the lads to show you around. He can show you where the bunk rooms are, and the canteen. Lunch is at twelve noon. Don't be late."

"Thank you, sir," said Sid. "I appreciate the opportunity, sir."

"Do you indeed? Good boy." Mr Ridgeway looked at Dad. "My compliments, Mr Everett. A well-mannered boy. That's very nice to see."

He pressed a bell on his desk, and Sid could hear it buzz out in the reception area. The lady who had been typing bustled into the room. "Yes, Mr Ridgeway?"

"Find Sam, would you please, Mrs Stanley?" said Mr Ridgeway. "Ask him to come and collect Sidney and show him around?" He smiled at Sid, holding out his hand. "Welcome aboard, Master Everett. Very pleased to have you."

Sid shook the hand extended towards him. It was a large hand with a firm grip, a bit like Mr Thorndon's. He hoped he would be able to do what they expected him to do.

Mr Ridgeway bent his head to murmur, "Sam's a decent boy. He'll show you where the bunkrooms are, and the canteen."

Sid started to thank him, but Mr Ridgeway was already turning away to shake hands with his dad.

Outside in the sunshine, Beryl and the twins gazed at him expectantly. Dad looked at Mum, and Sid realised that his family was going to leave straight away.

It seemed so sudden. He'd barely had any time with them, and now they were already going. He hugged Beryl, then hugged his mum for a bit longer. The twins were jumping up and down, yelling at him to come and visit soon and see their ferrets. Dad shook his hand again, and suddenly they were all in the car, driving away without him.

***

He stood waving, a sharp sense of loss sinking into his gut. As the curves of the gleaming black Morris Oxford disappeared around the bend in the driveway, footsteps crunched on the gravel behind him.

"Sidney Everett?" asked a sharp voice.

Sid turned to see a wiry boy with short, dark hair. "Yes. Are you Sam?"

"No. They couldn't find Sam, so they sent me," said the boy. "I'm Jim Carter. I suppose you're the boss's new pet?"

"What?" Sid couldn't believe his ears.

"You heard." Carter was around the same height as Sid, but older and more muscular. He had an aggressive chin, and the kind of eyes that instantly assess you and find you not quite up to the mark. He held out his hand. "Pleased to meet you," he said in a disdainful sort of way.

Sid had the distinct impression that he wasn't pleased at all. He shook Carter's hand. Carter's grip was hard, and Sid thought he detected a mean look in his eyes.

"Pleased to meet you, too," he said.

Carter's lip curled. "You might not be too pleased for too long." The mean look was now unmistakable. "I'll tell you straight off: pets aren't welcome here."

"Pets?" Sid could feel heat rising to his face.

"Yeah," said Carter. "You heard. Pets. Nothing wrong with your ears, anyway. Greasing up to the boss won't do you no good. Not here. Here, it's how well you ride, that counts. Not who your father is or who he knows."

"But..."

"Shut your mouth. And follow me."

Sid picked up his suitcase and followed, dismay filling his insides like icy water filling a bucket.

Chapter Six

Not A Warm Welcome

C arter set off at a cracking pace, and Sid followed, struggling to keep up with his heavy suitcase.

"Okay." Carter stopped abruptly, at a point where the gravel path divided into three. He spun around, pushing his face close to Sid's. "Nobody can see us here. And I want some answers."

Sid stared at him.

"You're from the North Island, aren't you?" snapped Carter.

"Yes," said Sid. "From Foxton." He set his suitcase down on the ground.

"Never heard of it," said Carter dismissively. "Who sent you here?"

"My boss, Mr Thorndon," said Sid. "He organised it."

"Yeah, but who organised it from here? I mean, did anyone here actually ask for you?"

"Mr Ridgeway, I think," said Sid. He tried to keep his voice steady despite the fury rising inside him. "He's a friend of Mr Thorndon's. I'm replacing somebody who broke his leg."

"I know you are," said Carter. "Supposedly. But we don't need you. Wade Daker's already been replaced."

"What?" said Sid.

"Someone has replaced him already." Carter spoke the words slowly and distinctly. "Me. I've replaced him. We don't need you."

"I don't understand," said Sid.

"Nor do I," said Carter. "And they're giving you Manawa. The whole thing stinks."

Sid glanced around, then back at Carter, trying to understand. "I don't know what's going on here," he said. "But you can't blame me for any of it. I'm just doing what I'm told."

"What a good boy," said Carter. "Well, what you've been told is wrong. You'll soon find out."

Sid narrowed his eyes. "You got a problem with me?"

"Only that you're here at all." Carter's face looked like it was carved out of stone.

Sid blinked. "Are you joking?"

"No," said Carter. "No joke. I know your old boss is Ridgeway's mate. It's the Old Boys Club. But I'm warning you. There's no cronyism here. No favourites. No rich people's pets. They promised me Manawa, and that's what's going to happen. Nothing's changing."

"Keep your hair on," said Sid. "I just got here. And I'd say the selection would be on merit."

"Yeah, on merit. But also on right. And who's got the right? I have. I've earned it." Carter kicked a lump of turf, sending it flying. "It makes me boiling mad," he said.

Sid stared at him. "Does it matter?" he asked.

"Yeah. It matters a lot. You're nobody special. You just keep your head down and your mouth shut. And don't try making yourself into a star. We don't want no prima donnas here." Carter glared. "And I'm not showing you around." He spat out the words. "You can find your own way to the bunk rooms. And the canteen's over there." He waved an arm vaguely. "Lunch is at twelve sharp. Be late, and you starve." He turned on his heel and stalked away.

***

Sid stared after him, running his fingers through his hair. He hadn't expected a red carpet, but he hadn't expected abuse either. He gazed around. Three paths. One of them must lead to the sleeping quarters.

The sound of cheerful whistling reached his ears, and a boy appeared, coming along one of the paths. The boy stopped whistling when he saw Sid. "Hello," he said. He had ginger hair and freckles, and a peeling, sunburned nose. "You look lost, standing there with your suitcase."

"I'm Sid. I just arrived."

"Welcome to Ridgeways," the boy said. "I'm Sam. Where are you off to?"

"Somebody called Carter was showing me the way to the bunk rooms. Then he suddenly got all mad at me, about me being here, and told me to find my own way."

"Oh, Jim Carter." Sam grimaced. "Carter's been going on about you for the last week. Winding himself up about how it isn't fair. How this new boy is going to have to watch himself."

"He certainly didn't seem pleased that I'm here," said Sid.

"You want to watch Carter," said Sam. "The head trainer is his uncle, and he makes sure everyone knows it."

"I don't care who his uncle is," said Sid. "I didn't ask to come here, but now I'm here, I'm going to make a go of it, and nobody's going to stop me."

"Shall I show you where the bunkrooms are?" asked Sam.

"Sure. Thanks." Sid picked up his suitcase.

"Follow me," said Sam.

As they walked, Sam questioned him. "Why *are* you here, if you don't mind my asking? Coming from the North Island and all. Everyone thinks you must be something pretty great on the racetrack. Did they send for you especially?"

Sid barked out a bitter laugh. "If you must know, they didn't ask for me. Not at all. My boss asked Mr Ridgeway to take me."

"Oh," said Sam. "Why was that?"

Sid glanced away, then back at the open, freckled face. "He was getting rid of me." The words were hard to say out loud. He looked at Sam, waiting for judgement, but Sam's face was full of concern.

"Crikey!" said Sam. "What did you do?"

"Nothing at all. Just his daughter's sort of like my girlfriend, I suppose. She's away at boarding school. But when she came home, well, we would have spent lots of time together."

"And he's making sure you won't," said Sam. "Not too keen on you, eh?"

"I guess not," said Sid. "He's always been good to me. More than fair. But it's sort of like a snobbery thing, I think. They're English. And they're rich."

"So what? It's a free country. And it's the 1940s, not the Middle Ages."

Sid was silent.

Sam grinned at him. "Cheer up. Here are the bunkrooms. I'm in this one." He pushed open the door, making it creak on its hinges.

Sid stepped inside. The bunk room was bigger than the one at the Thorndon's. Sunlight filtered in through a high window, and Sid could hear sparrows chirping and squabbling in the eaves. There were tall wooden bunks, a rug on the floor, and a small round table with a couple of old armchairs next to it.

"Not bad," said Sid. He grinned at Sam.

Each of the bunks had its personal touches – photos on the wall, colourful bedspreads. There were two empty bunks.

Sam pointed to a bunk in the corner that was a blaze of red. "That's mine," he said. He grinned. "My mum likes red. She made the quilt. And the extra cushion."

"That's nice," said Sid, feeling a pang. He didn't have any home-made quilt to spread out on his bunk bed. But he had some photos to stick on the wall. And the newspaper cuttings from his racetrack wins. He hadn't given them to his father.

Later, he thought.

"Pick a bed," said Sam. "The one above mine is empty."

Sid glanced up. A saggy kapok mattress hung over the end of the bunk like a blue and white striped waterfall, revealing a wooden slatted bed base. "Fine," he said. He scrambled up and heaved the mattress into place. He shook it hard to fluff it up, all ready to sink into at night.

Sam passed his bag up to him. "They'll give you sheets and blankets, and a quilt. It can get pretty cold here."

"And a pillow?" asked Sid.

"Of course," said Sam. "Two, if you ask."

A bell clanged in the distance.

"Lunch," said Sam. "Let's scarper."

Chapter Seven

Lunchtime Shock

Sid followed Sam into the dining room, noisy with loud voices and the scraping of chairs on the wooden floor. The air was fragrant with the smell of shepherds' pie and cabbage.

"Smells good," said Sid. He had to shout to hear himself over the hubbub of voices and the clatter of dishes and knives and forks.

He and Sam grabbed plates and lined up at the servery. A motherly-looking cook placed a large square of potato-topped pie on Sid's plate. "New, are you?" she asked.

"Hello, Mrs O'Brien. This is Sid, from Foxton," said Sam.

"Hello," said Sid.

Mrs O'Brien nodded. "Welcome to Ridgeways," she said.

A girl of around Sid's own age added a generous pile of cooked cabbage. She was wearing a white apron and had a scarf tied around her head. Her dark eyes sparkled as she noticed Sid. "The bread's at the end of the counter," she said. "You just help yourself."

Sid and Sam collected their cutlery and sat at a table near the window, their plates piled with shepherds' pie and cabbage and thick slices of white bread. A pat of butter on their table gleamed, with little drops of salt water beading on the top.

Sid looked back at where the cooks were serving lunch.

Sam followed his gaze. "That girl's name is Kiri," said Sam. "She's a kitchen hand. But she doesn't only work in the kitchen. She helps with the horses a bit, too."

"Helps with horses? How?" asked Sid.

"Dunno," said Sam. "Just helps. She helps our trainer. He's supposed to be retiring, but he's still here. He looks after any injured horses, too. Gets them back into condition. I think she helps with that."

"I haven't met any of the trainers."

"We've only got one. Mr Te Waka, but we call him Mr T. He's nice. You'll like him. Matt helps him too. He was a jockey, but he got too heavy for the horses, so now he helps with the training."

Sid looked over at Kiri again. "Does she ride?"

"What do you think?" said Sam. "Of course she rides. She's mad on horses. If girls could be jockeys, she'd be one." Sam laid his knife and fork across his empty plate and reached for his cup of tea. "Kiri can ride like the wind. She doesn't get paid to help with the horses – her actual job is in the kitchen. She helps because she loves horses."

"A nice life," said Sid.

"I suppose so," said Sam. "The kitchen's hard work. They start even earlier than we do. But when she's finished there, she's helping Mr T. Or else she just keeps to herself. Can't blame her, all these blokes here. She keeps out of our way."

Sid looked out of the window. In the distance, a track led away from the stables across the fields, avoiding the main driveway.

"Where does that track lead to?" he asked.

"What track?" asked Sam.

"Out there." Sid pointed.

"Oh," said Sam, "that goes to town, but it goes through the industrial area. We're not allowed to go that way. We're supposed to go to town a different way. That means we're only allowed to walk along the main road, which is rather boring."

A sudden hush fell over the room, and Sid looked up to see a grim-faced man standing in the doorway. His eyes were watchful, but Sid thought he had a strange air of excitement about him. He was a tall, bony man, like an older version of his father, with a craggy face, a hooked nose, and bushy eyebrows.

"MacDonald," Sam whispered. "The manager."

Everyone remained silent as Mr MacDonald strode to the front of the dining hall and stood facing them.

As he looked at the man's face, a chill ran down Sid's spine. He sat up straighter in his chair and kept his expression neutral.

"Good afternoon, everyone," growled Mr MacDonald.

"Good afternoon, Mr MacDonald," some of them muttered.

Almost like school, Sid thought.

Mr MacDonald gazed around, and the searchlight beam of his eyes found Sid. He smiled a thin, malicious smile and addressed the room. His voice was silky and menacing, but carried clearly to every corner in the uneasy silence.

"I won't hold you up, gentlemen. You're busy eating. I just thought I'd take this opportunity to introduce our newest arrival. A family friend of Mr Ridgeway himself. A boy who comes with glowing references." His mouth twisted into a sneer as his gaze fell again on Sid. "Stand up, Sidney Everett."

Sid leaped to his feet, his instincts screaming that something bad was about to happen.

MacDonald's voice changed to the ringing tone of an orator. "But that's not what counts here. Here, we're all equal. It's a fair race and a fair fight. The best horse and the best rider win. Not the one who has rich family connections. High-up, wealthy contacts. It's good riding that counts here. Hard work, and good riding."

Sid wanted to shout that it wasn't true. That he wasn't rich, and that he didn't know Mr Ridgeway from Adam. That his family connections were zero. But the words dried up on his tongue. How could he mention the most shameful thing of all, that he was here because Mr Thorndon wanted to get rid of him? With any possible answer frozen in his throat, he faced MacDonald, feeling like a rabbit caught in the headlights of a car.

He knew everyone was staring at him. All those eyes, looking at him, assessing him. Some faces were hard and scornful, obviously believing every word MacDonald had said. Others were frowning, puzzling things out.

"All right, chaps. As you were," MacDonald commanded.

Sid felt a tug on his sleeve.

"Sit down, mate," whispered Sam.

Sid dropped back onto his chair as the room filled again with the hum of voices.

Sam leaned over. "MacDonald's got a chip on his shoulder. 'The workers against the bosses.' All that left-wing stuff. He's a union man, and he always lets you know it."

Sid slumped in his chair. He remembered the railway station poster of David Copperfield. He felt just like the boy with a sign hanging around his neck saying "He bites." Only his sign, if he had one, would say "Boss's Pet".

Mr MacDonald suddenly loomed over him, his tall frame blocking the light from the window. "Everett?"

Sid kept his voice level, hoping not to betray the shock he was feeling. "Yes, Mr MacDonald?"

"Tomorrow morning, meet me at the track. Six o'clock sharp. I'll watch you do a trial ride on Lady Kate." He pursed his lips as if he'd tasted something sour. "You're to be riding Manawa, I'm told." He glanced at Sam, then looked back at Sid. "I'd like to see what you make of him. But I'll start you on Lady Kate. Sam here can show you where to find her. And where to meet me. And I'll see if you can actually ride." He spun on his heel and swept away.

Sid looked at Sam. "He's got it in for me, that's for sure."

"I dunno what his problem is," said Sam. "Well, he can't argue with skill. You just show him what you're made of. Show him you know one end of a horse from the other." He looked down at his empty plate, and then at Sid's full one. "Don't waste it – eat it. You'll need your strength."

Sid looked at his food, his stomach churning. He pushed his plate away. Suddenly, he couldn't face shepherds' pie and cabbage. Maybe he could eat the bread and butter. He picked up his cup of tea. "Tomorrow morning, eh? Yeah, I'll show him. I'll show him I can ride."

"That's the stuff," said Sam. "I'll help you get Lady Kate ready, and I'll take you to the track. And I'll hang around and watch from a distance. See how it goes."

"Thanks, Sam," said Sid. He was keen for a ride. But riding with MacDonald's eyes on him would not be fun, he was certain of that.

Chapter Eight

Riding for Mr MacDonald

Next morning, Sid shivered in the cool breeze as he waited at the track for Mr MacDonald. Sam stood next to him, holding Lady Kate's reins. High in the heavens, skylarks warbled as the sun lifted its white-gold rim above the horizon. It drenched the dun landscape, edging every blade of grass with fire.

Sid's heart lifted as the sun tipped the distant hills and dazzled him into being fully awake. Here he was – actually at Ridgeways, one of the most famous racing stables in New Zealand. He smiled at Sam. "Not a bad sunrise," he said. His fingers twisted together, betraying his anxiety.

"You'll be fine, mate," Sam said reassuringly. "You'll show them."

Lady Kate stamped a foot and snorted, her breath misting out into the chill air.

Sid looked around for Mr MacDonald. He should be here. In the distance, he heard a door bang shut. On the far side of the track, a figure emerged from one of the rear doors of the cook-house, and was moving swiftly along the track leading to town. It was the girl who worked in the kitchen. Kiri.

She wore a black cheese-cutter cap pulled down over her eyes. Her long hair streamed out behind her in the wind, and her red coat glowed in the early light. A bulging bag was slung over one shoulder. She glanced back once as she hurried along.

Was she going to town? Or the industrial area? And why would she go there? Sid looked at Sam, but he hadn't noticed Kiri. He was busy talking to Lady Kate and rubbing her neck. Sid almost said something, but changed his mind. A sixth sense told him that if there was something going on, keeping his mouth shut was best.

The nearby crunch of footsteps on the gravel made Sid spin around. Two men were approaching; their long, early shadows advancing before them along the path. The men crossed the short, dewy grass to join him and Sam. Sid's heart beat faster as he stood waiting. Their black silhouettes against the glowing apricot wash of the dawn sky made them seem sinister, like the bad guys at showdown time in a cowboy movie.

Sam handed him Lady Kate's reins. "Good luck," he whispered, and hurried away.

***

"Sidney?" Mr Ridgeway loomed large, the rising sun behind him throwing his face into a shadow so dark that Sid couldn't read his features. "This is Mr MacDonald, our manager." He turned to his companion. "This is the boy I told you about. Gerald speaks extremely highly of him. I'm hopeful he can replace Wade."

"We've met, already." MacDonald's hawk-like face twisted. His eyes, in the morning light, had a definite glint of malice.

"Good morning, sir." Sid studied Mr MacDonald.

Mr MacDonald rasped out, "How old are you?"

"Sixteen, Mr MacDonald," replied Sid.

"Done much riding?" MacDonald asked.

"Yes, sir. Quite a bit. I'm in the second year of my apprenticeship, and I'd done quite a lot of riding before that." Sid eyed him.

Surely he knows all this already, he thought.

Sid didn't bother to add that most of his riding before the apprenticeship had been on his old farm horse, Hugh. A plodder. And that some of it had been on his neighbour's horse, Silver – riding without permission on a wild beach at night. He blinked away the memory of the disastrous ending to his last beach ride.

Mr MacDonald glared at Sid. "We've lost a splendid rider. I suppose you think you're just as good?"

"I never said that, sir," answered Sid. "All I know is, they've asked me to ride his horse."

Mr MacDonald eyed Mr Ridgeway. "Let's see what he can do."

"I'll leave him in your hands, Mac," said Mr Ridgeway.

"Right you are," said Mr MacDonald. "I'll soon see what he's made of."

As Mr Ridgeway walked away, Mr MacDonald rounded on Sid, his eyes gleaming. "Before we start, let's get something clear."

His words had an ominous tone. Sid stared up at the manager's face, anxiety churning in the pit of his stomach.

Mr MacDonald snarled, "You listen to me, and you listen well."

Sid stared. He was listening. Obviously.

"I didn't want you here," said Mr MacDonald. "I told Mr Ridge-way we didn't need another boy. Wade Daker's an international standard, top jockey. He's one in a million. He's been racing all his life. An inexperienced boy can't possibly replace him." He glared at Sid. "I don't know what's going on, but it doesn't smell right to me. We've got jockeys here, and the best of the bunch is Jim Carter. We don't need an extra rider from some two-bit stable in Foxton."

Mr MacDonald leaned nearer, his nose looming close to Sid's face, and his thin lips twisting as he spoke. "But somehow, we have to put up with a Boss's Pet. A rich man's protégé. Well, it doesn't cut any ice with me. Not now, and not at any time. Like I told you, you get ahead on merit, here."

He put his face so close to Sid's that he could see the hairs in his nostrils and the stubble on his chin. His breath puffed into Sid's face. "You don't take shortcuts by sucking up to the bosses. Having rich parents. Being all friendly with the nobs. Good riding is what matters here. Not who your father is, or who you know."

"But I didn't..." Sid tried to defend himself.

"Don't answer back," snapped MacDonald.

"But my father isn't... And Mr Thorndon just..."

"Don't you DARE interrupt me when I'm speaking to you. Never! You understand?" MacDonald roared.

"Yes, Mr MacDonald," muttered Sid.

"Good." Mr MacDonald looked him up and down, his eyes full of fury. "I'm glad we've got that clear, you spoilt, smarmy little rat. You'll get no favours from me. Now you know how you stand." He raised his voice again. "Come on, then. Waste my day. Let's see you ride."

Sid completed his unfinished sentences in his head.

My father isn't a rich man. And Mr Thorndon was just getting rid of me.

He stumbled out onto the track, leading Lady Kate.

Chapter Nine

Not Too Shabby

Sid drew in a few deep breaths as he led Lady Kate onto the track, trying to calm himself. He could hear his blood pounding in his ears as adrenaline poured through his veins. How could he ride well, after the shock of being the target of so much hatred?

Focus on the horse, he told himself.

He halted Lady Kate, stroking her nose, murmuring a few words to connect with her. He breathed in her familiar, horsey smell. She was a sorrel mare with a white blaze down her nose. The gentle, common-sense aura that horses exuded made him feel better immediately. A steady confidence settled back into his heart. He swung himself up into the saddle, leaned over and patted her neck, admiring her thick mane and alert ears. Lady Kate was ready for what came next, he could tell. And now, so was he.

"Let's show him what we can do, eh, girl?"

Mr MacDonald stood at the fence, his stopwatch in his hand. "Lady Kate's got a lot of potential," he said. "What she needs is someone who can get the best out of her. As they all do."

Sid nodded. His mouth was dry. He wasn't used to being watched and assessed. He realised how lucky he'd been at the Thorndons'. The

Thorndons weren't exactly family friends, but they were neighbours – he'd known them all his life. And all the jockeys and staff there had been local.

"Can I give you a word of advice, boy?" said Mr MacDonald dryly.

"Yes?" Sid was startled.

"There's no time for dreaming."

"No, sir."

"You need to give it your best. Be attentive. There's a saying here," Mr MacDonald went on. "Focus or fail. I expect you to give your full attention to everything you do."

"Yes, sir," said Sid. He walked Lady Kate around in a circle and then lined her up on the track in front of Mr MacDonald. "Ready, Mr MacDonald."

"Just once around," said Mr MacDonald. He pressed his thumb down on his stopwatch, and shouted, "Now!"

Sid dug his heels into Lady Kate's sides and she shot off, her hooves thudding on the dry turf. He urged her on, picking up speed, and she flew around the track with an effortless ease that made his heart sing. He crouched in the saddle, urging her onward, feeling his excitement rising as the ground rushed dizzyingly beneath them.

Once around the track, and they passed Mr MacDonald at top speed, then Sid allowed Lady Kate to slow down. He took his time, turning her in a wide circle, then trotted back to Mr MacDonald.

"How did we go?" he asked.

"Not bad, son," said Mr MacDonald. "Not too shabby at all." He eyed Sid, a grudging respect in his eyes. "Twelve seconds a furlong. A good start. She's not used to you yet, and you're not used to her."

Sid waited.

"You'll do," he said shortly. "You'll earn your keep."

Sid hesitated. "Mr MacDonald?" he asked.

"Yes?"

"Am I riding in the Cup races? On Manawa?" Sid held his breath, waiting for Mr MacDonald to yell.

MacDonald didn't yell. "You haven't even met Manawa. He'd frighten the daylights out of you," he said, his words deliberate and distinct. "They choose you to ride in the Cup. That'd mean you'd have to be extremely good on a two mile gallop. You won't ride in the Cup on the strength of that little run. Not by a long chalk."

"I didn't expect that," said Sid.

Mr MacDonald snorted. "You're only here because some two-bit stable owner up north somewhere is friends with the boss."

Sid narrowed his eyes. "I've been riding for Thorndon Stables in Foxton," he said. "And on the Wanganui track. I've won some races."

Mr MacDonald eyed him. "So they tell me," he drawled. "But that won't be enough."

Sid stepped back. Mr MacDonald's face was going red.

"Mr Ridgeway's making a big mistake," spat MacDonald. "Gambling on a kid, just to please an old crony." His eyebrows came together in a bushy line. "A big mistake. And you made a big mistake coming down here."

"So what do I have to do?" asked Sid, trying to speak calmly.

"You do what you're told. Wait for an opportunity," said Mr Mac-Donald.

"When?" asked Sid. He knew he was pushing it. But he needed to know.

"The agents and the owners come and watch the early morning gallops," answered Mr MacDonald. "And there'll be a trial."

"Do I get to ride in the trial?"

Mr MacDonald didn't answer.

Sid waited, his anger rising. "I'm not expecting special treatment. I'm just asking."

Mr MacDonald's eyes gleamed. "You won't get any special treatment, I can assure you of that." He smirked. "How much do you know about Manawa?"

"Not much," said Sid. "I heard he's hard to handle."

"And the rest," said MacDonald. "He's a dangerous brute. The only one who can manage him is Wade Daker."

Sid waited for more, but MacDonald closed his mouth into a thin line and glanced around. He spotted a boy standing nearby. Sid spotted him, too.

Carter. What's he hanging around for?

Mr MacDonald's face lit up. "Ah, Jim. Here's somebody who knows how to ride."

The boy sauntered over to his uncle. He had the confident swagger of someone who knows they're in favour.

"Here's the new fella. Sidney Everett, from the North Island," said Mr MacDonald.

"We've met," said Carter, a sneer in his voice.

Mr MacDonald appeared not to notice it. "Well, I'll leave you two to make friends. You've got a bit of time before breakfast, Jim. You can show him how to put his horse away." He walked off, whistling.

"I'll do that," Carter murmured. He turned to Sid, a scowl on his face. "Follow me."

***

Carter led the way to the tack room. Sid followed, leading Lady Kate, his heart in his boots. Obviously, MacDonald would always favour his nephew. He'd probably been hoping all along that Carter would ride Manawa. How was he going to overcome that?

Carter stopped outside the tack room. "They must think I've got nothing better to do." His eyes narrowed. "I suppose you think you've impressed him. Well, you haven't. I can tell. You won't worm you way into my uncle's good books, he's not that easily shifted."

Two boys stepped out from the shadows of a building near the tack room.

"Ah," said Carter, grinning at them. "Allow me to introduce you to our budding new champion. He'll be riding Manawa, don't you know?" He glanced at Sid, and waved a hand at his mates. "Allow me to introduce Fred Walters."

A boy with hair so blond it was almost white stepped forward. "Delighted," he smirked.

"And this is Tyler. My good old mate, Tyler." Carter waved his hand in a courtly fashion. "From one of the best families."

All three boys guffawed loudly.

"Sidney Everett, chaps. From... where was it? Somewhere small. It's slipped my mind. Forgotten." He pushed his face close to Sid's. "Like you soon will be, Everett. Just a bit of an unpleasant smell in the air. Soon gone."

Carter spun around and began walking away. His two friends fell into step with him.

Sid watched them go.

Carter stopped suddenly, and turned back to glare at Sid. "And don't expect Wade Daker to be all over you, either."

Sid scratched Lady Kate behind the ears as he watched them saunter away. South Islanders were supposed to be a friendly lot. Not his experience so far. He heard a footstep behind him and turned. Sam was approaching, his good-natured, freckled face grinning.

"Well done!" said Sam. "I saw you ride." He glanced at the retreating backs of the three older jockeys. "Don't take any notice of them. They're the foul smell, around here." He reached out a hand and stroked Lady Kate's nose. "Lady Kate, you beauty!" He looked at Sid. "You impressed him. MacDonald never likes to let on if he's actually pleased with anything." He paused. "Need a hand? It's almost breakfast time. You don't want to be late."

"Thanks!" said Sid.

Sam helped unsaddle Lady Kate. Sid lugged the saddle into the tack room, his footsteps thudding on the wooden floor. He inhaled the familiar aroma of leather and polish. Two long rows of saddles stretched into the distant shadows, gleaming softly in the dim light. He found Lady Kate's name on the wall and heaved her saddle onto the twin wooden rods below it.

He turned back. Sam waited, silhouetted against the light.

Sam called. "Hurry up. Let's turn her out into the paddock and get to breakfast before the bacon's all gone."

As they passed the office, the office lady came outside and called after them.

"Sidney Everett?"

Sid stopped and turned around. "Yes?"

"You've got a message." She waved a small piece of paper.

Sid's heart leaped. He jogged over to her.

"From my family?" he asked.

"Yes. Your father rang. He's coming to pick you up tomorrow morning, to take you home for the day. Mr Ridgeway has agreed to it, so you don't need to worry about that."

"Oh!" Sid took the slip of paper from her outstretched hand and opened it.

In neat writing, it said 'A Day on the farm. Picking you up at eight o'clock tomorrow morning. Dad.'

He beamed. "Thank you!" he said.

Chapter Ten

Greaseball

The next morning, Sid woke extra early. Excitement flooded through him as he remembered what day it was. Today, his family was coming to pick him up and take him home.

A gentle snore drifted up from the bunk below. Sid peered over the edge of his bunk to where Sam's sleeping form lay sprawled out. He scrambled down to the ground, avoiding stepping on Sam's out-flung arm. He dressed quickly and slipped outside into the pre-dawn chill.

Outside, it was still dark. Somewhere in the distance, a dog barked. There was no wind at all, and the far-off clang of a tram travelled clearly on the still air. A billion stars sparkled in the velvet darkness of the sky. On the horizon, the pale lemon of early dawn was just perceptible.

Sid headed for the cookhouse, following the tantalising aroma of toast. As he approached, the lawn glittered with silver dewdrops in the light from the kitchen windows.

He closed the cookhouse door quietly behind him. The dining tables stretched out long and bare in the empty room. It was a haven of warmth and quiet, apart from the hum of refrigerators.

Sid tiptoed towards the hatch where the food was served, the wooden slatted screen pulled down. He could hear the cooks conversing in the kitchen on the other side of the hatch. An enormous pot of tea stood waiting on the tea trolley. That was handy. He poured himself a cup and added milk. Then he sat by the window, wondering if he'd see Kiri pass by as he had yesterday morning.

Probably far too early, he told himself.

He wondered what she had been carrying, and where she was going to. Nobody else seemed to take any notice. Were they not observant? Or did everyone know what she was up to?

Sid sipped his tea. He was curious. And actually, he'd like to get to know her. Just as a friend, of course. His loyalty was to Sarah, at boarding school in far-off Wellington.

Sarah. He hadn't had a letter from her since he'd left the Thorndons'. Anxiety tap-danced inside him, but he squashed it down. She was busy. So was he. And letters take a long time to write. And a long time to travel through the post.

The kitchen hatchway slid up, and the smiling face of Mrs O'Brien, the cook, appeared. Sid noticed Kiri behind her, wearing kitchen overalls, reading a newspaper that lay spread out on one of the long sideboards.

Mrs O'Brien's eyes twinkled at him. "You're early, dear," she said.

"My family's coming today," said Sid. He left his seat by the window and went over to the servery.

"That's nice," said Mrs O'Brien. "That's a long way to travel."

"They live here," said Sid. "At Rangiora. They moved down here nearly a year ago. I haven't even seen their place yet."

"You must be excited," said Mrs O'Brien. "You're a bit early for breakfast. But we can make you some toast. Would you like that?"

"Yes, please," said Sid.

Mrs O'Brien turned away and went over to where Kiri was studying the newspaper. "What are you looking at, young lady?"

Kiri jumped.

Mrs O'Brien leaned over Kiri's shoulder, clicking her tongue disapprovingly. "Looking at horoscopes! You shouldn't be looking at those. It's a sin. I need some toast."

"I'm looking at the personal column. It happens to be next to the horoscopes, that's all." Kiri tried to close the newspaper, but Mrs O'Brien snatched it up.

"I'll have that." The cook held the paper aloft. "I don't mind, really, dear. I even have a peek at the stars myself, sometimes. But your mother wouldn't like you reading them. I know that. She'd be cross. Can you make some toast now, please Missy, for the young man here, and I'll have a nosy at the personals myself."

She spread out the newspaper on the bench as Kiri moved away.

"Oooh, look! Here's one for a missing husband," said Mrs O'Brien. She barked out a short laugh. "What a hope!" She held up the newspaper and read aloud. "Missing. Where are you, Daniel?" She gasped and looked up, her broad face filling with dismay. "Crikey, Kiri! It's for Daniel Connolley! She's advertising for him!"

Sid noticed that Kiri's usually brown face had gone quite white.

Mrs O'Brien kept reading. "Disappeared suddenly Dunedin. If anyone has seen him, please contact the writer. Come home, my love. Iris." She put her hand over her mouth, then pulled it away. "Crikey," she said again. "It's Iris. The poor dear."

Kiri shook her head. "Shhh, Mrs O'Brien!" She eyed Sid meaningfully.

Mrs O'Brien instantly recovered herself. She folded up the newspaper with dignity and came back to Sid. "Your toast won't be a minute, young man."

"Thank you," said Sid.

"Kiri," Mrs O'Brien called over her shoulder. "Get a move on with that toast."

Sid stood at the counter waiting for his toast, puzzling over what he'd just heard. The missing soldier he'd seen in the newspaper at the station. It must be the same man.

Mind your own business, Beryl would say. Keep your nose clean.

"Toast's ready." Kiri appeared at the counter with a plate in her hand, stacked high with warm, golden-brown toast. Her hand shook as she held out the plate. "There's jam and Marmite on the sideboard." Her voice was husky. She cleared her throat, watching Sid nervously.

"Thank you." Sid took the plate of toast.

The girl smiled. "How are you settling in?"

Sid suddenly couldn't think of anything to say. "Good," he muttered.

"I'm Kiri," the girl continued.

"I'm Sid," said Sid. "Sid Everett. I'm still finding my way around." He hesitated. "It's a big place here."

"Always something happening," she said. "It's an interesting place to work." She smiled again.

Sid thought she had the nicest smile he'd ever seen. Apart from Sarah's, of course.

"How long have you worked here?" he asked.

"Oh, a few months," Kiri said vaguely. "What about you? Where are you from? Not around here."

"Foxton," said Sid, his throat suddenly constricting at the memory of home. A memory he'd been avoiding. He tried not to think about it, but now it grabbed him, and it hurt.

"Where's that?" she asked.

"In the North Island. On the west coast."

"Oh. Welcome to the Mainland. I'll let you eat your toast before it gets cold." She smiled again and turned back to the warmly lit kitchen.

Sid took his plate of toast back to his table by the window, then went to the sideboard for some jam and Marmite. There was no butter.

He returned to the counter. Mrs O'Brien and Kiri seemed to be having a heated, but whispered, conversation. He cleared his throat, and Kiri glanced up, then came over.

"Can I please have some butter?" he asked.

"Oh, yes, of course." Kiri went to a wooden trolley at the centre of the kitchen where small, white china plates holding pats of butter were laid out, ready to take to the tables. She handed him a plate. "Here you go." She eyed him anxiously. "You didn't hear what we were talking about earlier, did you?"

"About what?"

"Something in the paper."

"Didn't hear a word," he said. He was pretty sure she knew that wasn't true. That he'd heard everything they'd said.

"Very good." She gave him a wink.

Sid returned to his table with the butter, feeling more curious than ever.

What was it about the missing Daniel Connolley?

Oh well, he told himself. It was nothing to do with him. He had more important things to worry about. He had a horse racing career ahead of him. That goal needed all his focus. He buttered his toast and was taking a big bite when the door burst open. A trio of older jockeys swaggered in, dressed in smart clothes, ready for town. Carter was in the centre. Of course.

The boys eyed him, and one of them said something in a voice that was too low for Sid to hear. They all sniggered.

Sid looked away, feeling his pulse rate speed up. What were they saying about him? Something derogatory. He sipped his tea and realised he'd forgotten to put sugar in.

He hesitated. If he went over to get sugar, he'd attract more of their attention. Oh well. They didn't scare him. But he hated being laughed at. He got to his feet, pushing his chair back, hearing it scrape loudly on the wooden floor.

The trio of jockeys at the counter stopped laughing. They stared in silence as Sid crossed the canteen floor.

Feeling their eyes watching him, Sid scooped up a spoonful of sugar and dumped it into his cup. He stirred his tea, listening for any word they might say.

At first, he heard nothing. He returned to his table, aware of their stares following him, and sat down. Then one of them muttered something, and all three burst into raucous laughter.

"Pooo-weeee!" said one boy. "There's a bad smell in here."

Sid remembered his name. Tyler.

"Yeah," said Fred Walters, the boy with the white-blond hair. "A bit of a stink. The stink of dirty, rotten grease."

Tyler shouted, "Hey, Greaseball!"

Sid kept his eyes on his plate. His mouth was dry. He didn't want to look up.

Tyler shouted again. "Hey, Greaseball. I'm talking to you."

Sid looked up.

Tyler was staring at him. "Greasing up to the bosses. It won't help you here, mate. Some of us have been here a long time, just getting on with our jobs. We don't like slimy little rich boys greasing their way in."

Sid took a careful breath. "I'm not rich," he said. "And I'm not a greaser. I'm a jockey, same as you. I ride. That's all."

"Yeah, right." The other boy seemed to grow bigger by the second. "Your Daddy just happens to know old Ridgeway. Very pally."

"That's not true!" Sid pushed back his chair and stood up. "My dad doesn't know him. My old boss knows him. But I'm not here because anybody's trying to do me a favour."

Carter leaned back against the servery counter, stretching out his legs. "Really? Looks like favouritism to me." He paused. "Why are you here, then? Getting rid of you, were they?"

Sid froze.

Carter smirked when he saw he'd made a good guess. "Aha! Now we're getting near the truth, eh? But you're still a greaser. Playing on your connections. It won't wash here, Greaseball."

Sid opened his mouth, then stopped. He didn't want to tell anybody the truth. That they'd shunted him off to the South Island with no option. No way was he going to share that kind of information with anybody here.

He straightened his shoulders. "I'm here to ride, that's all. I'm here to win races." He left his tea and toast on the table and walked to the door, expecting any moment that footsteps would follow him, that somebody would grab him.

A rush of footsteps alerted him. Sid spun around.

Carter grinned and stepped around him, swinging the canteen door wide. "Just opening the door for you, mate."

"You want a go?" said Sid. "Just step outside, and you've got it."

"What, fisticuffs?" The boy raised his eyebrows. "I'll certainly give you the pleasure. But not right now. I'm on my way to town. Don't want to mess up my clothes." He held the door open. "Another time. Off you go, Greaseball."

Sid stepped through the doorway. Carter's foot shot out, catching his ankle. Sid tripped and stumbled, falling down the steps onto the pavement outside. A sharp pain stabbed his knee.

Picking himself up, he turned to glare up at Carter. "Any time," he said. "Any time. I don't mind a bit of dust."

"Might stick to the grease," said Carter. He stood with his hands on his hips, a mocking grin on his face.

Sid, his face burning with fury, turned away. He strode out into the growing daylight, refusing to limp, despite the pain in his knee, inhaling big gulps of crisp morning air.

Chapter Eleven

Horse Therapy

Sid hurried away, grateful for the fresh morning breeze cooling his burning face. His heart was pounding. His trousers stuck to his bleeding knee. It was still too early for his dad to arrive. Ignoring the pain, he strode off to where the horses were grazing. A bit of horse company was what he needed.

He reached the first paddock, breathing hard. The peaceful sound of horses munching grass brought back memories of home. Birds chirped, and leaves rustled in the morning breeze. Sid felt his heart rate slowing. Being around horses was calming. He breathed in their comforting smell and the fragrance of the dewy turf.

A splash of colour on the far side of the paddock caught his eye. An older man was in the paddock with one of the horses, stroking her nose and talking to her. She was a striking looking horse – dark brown with white spots and splashes on her hindquarters.

Appaloosa, thought Sid. *You don't see many of those.*

The man looked up as Sid arrived. His eyes were dark and keen, and his chin jutted forward. His shirt sleeves were rolled up and a battered felt hat shaded his face.

Sid leaned on the fence rail, the wood still cool and damp from the chill of the night. "Good morning," he said.

"Mōrena, young man. I haven't seen you here before. You must be that Sidney Everett they're all talking about."

"I'm Sid," said Sid. "Yeah, I know they've been talking about me. But it's not true, what they're saying."

"I'd believe that," said the man. "I'm Henry Te Waka, the trainer here. If they tell you to look for the old fella, that's me. Or you can call me Mr T. They all call me Mr T."

"Pleased to meet you," said Sid.

Mr T looked at the knee of Sid's trousers, where blood had soaked through. "Want something on that?"

"No, it's fine."

Mr Te Waka eyed him. "Don't let it get you down," he said. "These things get started and they're very hard to stop. The only thing to do is just be yourself. Once they get to know you, they'll change their tune. Then they'll want to know the truth."

Sid wasn't so sure. "What's her name?" he asked, changing the subject.

"Paint," said Mr Te Waka. "She's my own horse. She's not a racehorse, although she's pretty speedy." He indicated a slender palomino grazing next to Paint. "And this is Filigree. She's been in recovery. She took a tumble, but she's right as rain now. She just needs to get her confidence back."

"Nice name," said Sid. He hesitated. "I could help. If you need any help, that is."

Mr T studied him, assessing him. "Come in here and say hello to her."

Sid climbed over the fence, his knee smarting as he did so, and joined the trainer. "Filigree, eh?" he said. "You're a beautiful girl." He stroked her neck. "Soon be back on the track, eh? And going like the wind."

"Had a lot to do with horses?" asked Mr T. "Besides racing, I mean?"

"We've had a horse at home all my life. Old Hugh. My brothers and I used to ride him to the river. We rode him all over the place. And I was at a racing stable in Foxton, before I came here."

"You've got kind hands," said Mr T. "I always notice people's hands. How they touch a horse. Gentle hands."

He held out his hands for Sid to see. They were brown, plump, and a little wrinkled with age. Sid noticed his pinkie fingers, particularly. Something had made the little finger crooked on each hand.

"Know what that's from?" asked Mr T.

"No," said Sid.

"It's from holding the reins," said Mr Te Waka. "I slip the reins around my little fingers as I hold them. That's all the pressure you need. If it's too much for your little fingers, it's too much for the horse."

"Wow," said Sid. "I haven't heard that before."

"Done any actual training of a horse?" asked Mr T.

"No," said Sid. "Not actual training. But I looked after a horse after an injury. Got him back to full strength."

Mr T smiled. "I'd be glad to have your help. If you have the time. I wouldn't mind a bit of assistance."

"Thanks, Mr T. I'd like that." It would be a relief to have somewhere to go that wasn't around the other jockeys. Then Sid remembered *why* he'd had to look after Silver. He felt his face burn.

"I have to tell you something, Mr Te Waka. That horse I helped get his confidence back. I'm the one who caused his accident."

Mr Te Waka studied Sid's face, his expression kind. "Thank you for your honesty, young man," he said. "That's alright. Accidents happen. And we all make mistakes. You're lucky you had the chance to fix things up."

"That's true," said Sid. "I was lucky. Not everybody gets that chance."

"You're an honest boy," said Mr T. "I like that. It's not a common trait. Most people try to pretend they never did anything wrong."

Sid didn't know how to answer that.

Mr Te Waka smiled at him. It was a slow, gentle smile that made his eyes crinkle up at the corners. "You're young; you've got all your life ahead of you. Things never go right all of the time. But if you do your best, you'll mostly come out on top. And if you can admit your mistakes, you're halfway there already."

He reached out and stroked Filigree's shining neck. "Especially around horses. Be honest with horses. They're honest animals. They don't trick you." He studied Sid, his eyes assessing him. "You seem to have your head screwed on right. And you like horses, don't you?"

"Of course," said Sid.

"I mean, just for themselves," said Mr Te Waka.

Sid thought about Hugh, his old farm horse, and how he used to ride him over the hills and down to the river to swim. And the many times he'd gone out to the paddock just to hug Hugh, and breathe in the warm, comforting smell of horse.

"Yup," he said. "I know what you mean."

Mr T nodded slowly. "I knew you would. Some kids these days, they've got no idea. Even some of these jockeys. They see it as a job, that's all. And lots of kids have never even been near a horse. A bit of time with horses would do them the world of good."

"You mean, learning to ride?" Sid was puzzled.

"No, I mean to just spend time with them. Kids nowadays are getting wild. Or else they're unhappy about something. Life's different to how it used to be before the war. Being around horses could help them."

Mr Te Waka rubbed his chin thoughtfully. "For example, I've got a boy here now, staying with his relatives. His home life is... well, it isn't the best it could be. He comes here and spends time with the horses. Brushing them, walking them around. Being near them. I haven't suggested riding. If he wants to, of course he can, and I'll help him. But right now, spending time around horses is doing him the world of good." He shook his head sadly. "There are a lot of unhappy kids out there these days. And a lot of troubled men. Especially since the war."

Sid thought of his dad. "True," he said.

Dad!

"I've gotta go, Mr T," he said. "My dad's coming to pick me up. He might be here already."

Mr Te Waka lifted his chin in assent. "See you again, son," he said.

Sid raced across the paddock, dodging the horses, trying to ignore the stinging of his knee. He vaulted over the wooden fence, hurried to his bunk room and changed his trousers so his mother wouldn't say anything, then jogged down to the parking area in front of the main building.

His dad's shiny black car was approaching along the driveway. Dad would be keen to hear about life at Ridgeways. Sid's stomach clenched at the thought of describing life at Ridgeways.

I'll just tell him the good bits, he decided.

And Dad would be keen to know about what races were coming up, and which races he might ride in. He wouldn't be interested in hearing about how horses can help unhappy kids.

He shook his head, trying to shake out all that horse-therapy stuff Mr Te Waka had put in there. All that talk about needy kids and troubled ex-soldiers.

I'm not here for that. I'm here to ride. And to win. That's all that matters.

Tyres crunched on the gravel as Dad's car pulled up in front of him. Sid saw his father's face grinning at him through the windscreen. He could see some other people in the car, too. Mum and the twins.

Sid rushed over and pulled open the front passenger door.

"Hello, Mum," he said.

"Hello, Sidney," said Mum.

"Hello, son," said Dad. "They've come for a tour. A quick look around, then we'll take you home."

Chapter Twelve

A Tour of the Stables

Mum stepped out of the car. Sid thought she looked younger and prettier than he remembered. And a lot happier.

"Sidney!" Mum swept him into a hug that made him realise a hug was something he'd missed very much.

When she let him go, she looked into his eyes with her familiar, searching gaze. "Are you keeping well, son? Are they feeding you well?"

"Yes, Mum, I'm fine. And the food is great." Sid wasn't going to mention the nastiness. The way most of them treated him like dirt. "You can't be late for breakfast though, or you'll miss out on the bacon. But there's always plenty of everything else."

"Well, that sounds all right," said Mum. She studied him. "You look different, somehow. But of course, you're growing up."

"Bacon for breakfast?" It was Dad, beaming from ear to ear. "You're doing all right then, Sidney. Bacon for breakfast!"

Sid's eyes met his father's and a current of understanding seemed to travel through the air between them. He and Dad hadn't always seen eye to eye, but now they were close.

"Sid, Sid! Can we have a look around?" The twins were shouting, as usual.

"I suppose it would be all right," said Sid.

Feeling a little embarrassed, he set off towards the cookhouse with his parents and two brothers behind him. He hoped Carter and his mates were gone.

The kitchen was busy as breakfast was being served. Carter and his buddies seemed to have disappeared. Mrs O'Brien waved to Sid through the servery window. Kiri also waved. Sid felt his cheeks heating as he waved back.

His brothers missed nothing. "Who's she, Sid?" asked Bruce, as Sid led his family outside and away from the canteen. "Your new girlfriend?"

"Girlfriend?" said Dad. Dad never missed a thing either. "There'll be no girlfriends for Sid at the moment. Far too busy training to be a jockey, aren't you, Sidney?"

"Yes," said Sid, glaring at his brothers.

"What about Sarah?" asked Mum. "Are you still writing to Sarah, Sidney?"

"Yup," said Sid. His heart sank. How was it they all knew his business? And what made them think it was fine to talk about it?

A distant barking and baying of dogs drew his father's attention.

"Got dogs here? Hunting dogs?" he asked.

"I dunno," said Sid. "Just horses, as far as I know."

"Sounds like dogs," said Dad.

"Come on," said Sid. "I'll show you my bunk room."

He led them across the yard to the bunk rooms. A murmur of voices and bursts of laughter came from the long, low-lying building as they approached.

"That's where I sleep, in there." He pointed to one door. "But we won't go in. I just realised – they'll be getting dressed." He'd hoped to introduce them to Sam, but best not to barge in. Not with his mum, anyhow.

He led them past the wide sweep of the training track and followed the path to the stables. Off to one side, a house sat back from the path, with a high, unpainted picket fence around it. It was Mr MacDonald's house, Sam had told him. The dogs had to be here. Sid shivered. This house gave him the creeps. Although there was nothing actually creepy about it. It was the usual small villa, with a bay window at the front, on one side, and a small veranda. But it had a bad feeling. Sid usually tried to hurry past.

Two large dogs rushed out, hurling themselves at the fence and unleashing a volley of ferocious barks and growls. Mum backed away, and the twins moved closer to their dad.

Sid was relieved to see that MacDonald had shut the gate. He studied the dogs, barking and jumping up at the fence. He hadn't seen them before, ever. Maybe they were usually tied up around the back?

"Pig dogs," said Dad. "Bred for hunting."

"They look really mean," whispered Mum.

"They'll bail up a pig, and wait for the hunter to come and kill it," said Dad. "They're trained to do that. They shouldn't attack a person."

The dogs growled and snarled at him through the fence.

"But I wouldn't want to test that out," said Dad. He turned to Sid. "Lead on, son."

Sid led the way further along the gravel path to the stables, and the family followed, the barks and growls of the dogs fading behind them.

The stable was already Sid's favourite place at Ridgeway's. He un-latched the door, and stepped quietly into the horsey, hay-scented gloom, his family following close behind.

The horses stood in their stalls, their ears pricked at the sound of someone's approach.

"Wow!" Bill was as much of a horse lover as Sid was. "So many of them. They're beautiful."

"This is Lady Kate," said Sid.

Bill reached up a hand to stroke Lady Kate's velvet nose.

A gleaming black horse stamped and snorted. The name above his stall was 'Manawa'.

Manawa. Sid's heart leaped and sank at the same time. This was the horse he was supposed to ride.

"Dad?" said Sid. "This is Manawa. Ridgeway's top horse. He was bred here, and he belongs to Mr Ridgeway. He'll be in the New Zealand Cup Race." He hesitated. "All he needs is a rider."

"So I hear," said Dad. "And that's what you're here for, eh?"

"Yup. Apparently."

"That's a famous name," said Dad.

"Yeah," said Sid. "He's won a lot of races." He hesitated. "Dad?"

"Yes, son?"

"They think I'm some sort of horse expert. Mr Thorndon told them that's what I am."

"And Manawa needs a horse expert?"

"Most people can't get near him." Sid shrugged. "I haven't tried. I was told to wait for Mr Daker. And he hasn't been here."

Mum held out her hand, and the horse nuzzled her open palm. "He doesn't seem too bad to me," she said.

"So, Dad, here's the thing," said Sid. "I haven't actually ridden him yet. I think he likes me. But there's not much time left before the Cup."

"So you need to get on with bonding with him," said Dad.

"Yes," said Sid.

"Can't you choose which horse you ride?" asked Bill.

"No," said Sid. "You don't get to choose. They tell you which one you're riding. They watch you, and see which horses you're good with. I've been told I'm riding Manawa, without riding him even once." He shrugged. "I just wish Mr Daker would hurry up. If Manawa likes me, it's my big chance."

"Is it the only chance?" asked Mum.

"No," admitted Sid. "But for this year, it might be." He frowned. "To be honest, nobody really tells me much. It's different here. Not like Foxton or Wanganui. It's bigger. And there's a lot of money involved. You can feel it."

"Yes," said Dad. "It feels rich."

"And some people here don't want me riding him," said Sid. "They've made that pretty clear." He had blurted it out. He waited, holding his breath, to see what his dad would say.

Dad gave him a reassuring smile. "Take no notice of them. Mr Ridgeway didn't strike me as the sort of man to let other people tell him what to do with one of his horses."

Sid laughed, feeling a weight lift off his shoulders. "You're right, Dad. He's not."

"He's a very nice horse, Sidney." Dad reached up a hand and stroked Manawa's velvet nose.

The horse dipped his head and nuzzled Dad's shoulder.

"He likes you, Dad," said Sid. He'd always admired his dad's gentle way with horses. Dad was a natural.

Dad turned away from the horse, his face glowing. "Very nice horse indeed. And you're riding him. What a privilege!" He looked at his family. "Well, what are we waiting for?" he said. "Let's take Sid home. Are you ready, Sidney?"

Home, thought Sid. Not the old home they'd left behind in the North Island. A new home he hadn't yet seen, where his brothers lived a life he'd never experienced.

"Yup," said Sid. "I sure am."

Dad led them all back out into the sunshine.

Chapter Thirteen

Home

S id latched the stable door and followed his parents and younger brothers to the waiting car. It wasn't a long drive from Ridgeways to Rangiora. Sid looked out at the changing view, trying to adjust to being in a new place. It was a strange mix – the unfamiliar landscape outside, and inside the car, the family he knew so well. They passed through the city and headed out along country roads again. Finally, the car slowed.

"Here we are," said Dad.

They turned off the road onto a winding driveway, bumpy with ruts and corrugations of sun-baked earth. Sid rolled down his car window and dust billowed in. As the car lumbered down the hill, Sid saw the house and his face broke into a huge smile. It was a sprawling, weather-board villa with yellow painted walls and a red corrugated iron roof.

"This looks nice," said Sid.

Dad pulled up in front of the house and turned off the engine. They were in a sparkling green valley filled with birdsong. Sid could hear the faint sound of rushing water from a stream somewhere. A starling on the chimney pot burst into song. And there on the veranda was Jess, the family dog, stretching and wagging her tail, her bright eyes fixed hopefully on the car.

Sid opened his door and climbed out, and Jess launched herself off the veranda with a volley of joyful barks, and flew at him in a flurry of fur and whiskers and a madly waving tail.

"Jess!" cried Sid, crouching down to hug her. He let her lick his face and hands, something he'd always tried to avoid. "Jess!" Jess's tail thumped against his legs as he stood up again. He beamed. "Does she like it here?"

"What do you think?" asked Mum.

"I'd say yes," laughed Sid. He kept on stroking her head as he looked around.

"We were lucky," said Dad. "Our five acres got carved off from the big farm, along with one of the farm workers' houses."

Mum climbed out of the car. "Very nice for a farm cottage," she said. "The main farmhouse is that big brick house we passed just up the road."

Bill and Bruce raced to a small wooden hut perched high on tall posts. "Come on, Sid! These are our ferrets! Sid, come and look!"

Sid peered into the small, wire-fronted cage. It seemed empty. He could see a sleeping box at the back, and he supposed the ferrets were in there. The whole thing had a strong, unpleasant smell.

"They pong," said Bruce. "But you get used to it." He tapped on the front of the cage and took a piece of biscuit from his pocket. "They like this. They prefer meat, they're meat eaters. But a bit of biscuit is like a treat for them." He poked the biscuit through the wire mesh.

Sid watched, fascinated, as a small, lithe animal slipped out from the sleeping box, its movements silent and sinuous. Its fur was cream and brown, and its beady black eyes seemed to have a wicked glint.

"This is Foxy," said Bruce. "He's mine."

The ferret took the piece of biscuit and ate it quickly and neatly, its bright eyes and white teeth gleaming. Then it pulled itself up against the wire, looking for more. A second ferret slunk out, its head weaving from side to side, eyes alert. It had darker fur and was slightly smaller.

"This is my one," said Bill. "This is Finch."

"They stink," said Sid. "Why do you keep them?"

"Why?" Bill stared at him. "We told you. To catch rabbits, of course. We've got snares, and we get tons of rabbits. You put the ferret down the rabbit hole, the rabbits run out, and bingo! You've got them. The farmers round here pay you money to get rid of them."

"And we sell the skins," said Bruce. "And Mum makes rabbit stew. It's really nice."

"Tastes like chicken," said Bill. "Kind of."

Mum called from the house, "Boooys!"

Sid looked at his brothers. "Breakfast?"

"Yeah, I think so." Bill took out another piece of biscuit, broke it in half, and poked it through the wires. "Have you had breakfast?"

"Only a bit of toast," said Sid, and then remembered he hadn't eaten his toast. Or drunk his tea. His tummy rumbled and his knee hurt.

The ferrets nipped off pieces of biscuit. Sid caught glimpses of their small pink tongues and wickedly sharp teeth. The biscuit was soon gone.

"You'll have to come rabbiting with us," said Bill. "You'd love it."

Sid wasn't so sure.

"Come on," said Bruce. "Breakfast!"

The twins raced to the house. Sid followed more slowly, Jess at his side. His bloody knee had dried now, but it felt stiff. He was glad that his clean trousers hid his knee, so he wouldn't have to answer any questions.

***

The kitchen was cosy with the heat from the coal range, and the morning sun streamed in through a small window above the sink. Mum was warming the teapot. Dad was at the table, cutting slices of bread from a fat, golden-crusted loaf and stacking them in a pile.

Mum had set out the familiar blue and white china plates on the table with knives and forks, but there were only five of them. Sid felt a lump in his throat as he looked at the five plates. There had always been seven. But now Beryl was away at teachers' training college, and Ruby was at deaf school.

"Do you want any help, Mum?" he asked.

"It's all done, Sidney. You just wash your hands and sit down at the table." She glanced at Bill and Bruce. "Boys? You'd better do a thorough job of washing those hands if you've been touching the ferrets."

"We weren't touching them, Mum. We were just giving them bits of biscuit."

"Wash them anyway and then sit at the table."

Mum brought a steaming plate of fried potatoes and crispy bacon to the table and went back for the eggs. "Our own eggs, Sidney. We got some more chickens. They're good layers."

She brought an extra plate to the table, put some food on it, and began cutting up bacon and potatoes and eggs into small pieces.

"What are you doing, Mum?" asked Sid.

"This is for Auntie Glad," said Mum.

"Auntie Glad?" asked Sid.

"She's my second cousin," said Mum. "But everyone calls her Auntie Glad. She's really a Gladys, but Glad for short."

She chopped the food a bit more. "When we moved down here, I started getting in touch with all my family. There aren't many living in this area now, but Auntie Glad was still here. She'd just had a fall, and she was in hospital, and they weren't letting her go back home alone. The doctors don't like people living all on their own after they've had a fall. They think they won't manage. Chances are, they would have put Auntie Glad in a home, and she hated that idea. She didn't want to go. So, Dad and I said we'd have her here. Didn't we, Arthur?"

"Yes," said Dad. "Not that there was anything wrong with the old people's home. She just wasn't the sort to go there, that's all. Too independent."

"I didn't even know we had an Auntie Glad," said Sid.

"You've got lots of aunties and uncles down here that you've never met," said Mum. "This is where I grew up. When we moved here, they were all talking about what to do with Aunt Gladys. And it just turned out that I was the right one to take her in. It almost seemed like it was meant to be – us coming here just in time to look after her."

She put the plate of food on a tray and added a cup of tea in a dainty china cup and saucer. "She'll get up and come out when it's a bit warmer. I think she'll be keen to meet you, Sidney. Do you want to come with me now?"

"Of course," said Sid.

Chapter Fourteen

Auntie Glad

Mum picked up the tray and Sid followed her out of the kitchen. She tapped on a bedroom door. "Good morning, Glad," she called, pushing the door open.

"Good morning, Mary." Auntie Glad had a bright, chirpy voice. "A lovely morning!"

Sid followed his mother into the bedroom. The room was dim and quiet, with flowery wallpaper and a high ceiling. It was full of lingering shadows, despite the mellow light pouring in through the window. In the stillness, Sid could hear that Auntie Glad was breathing in a raspy sort of way. The curtains were open, and the blind was halfway up, letting the soft sunshine spread a golden square on the dark wooden floor.

Auntie Glad was sitting upright in a tall, single bed with wooden bed ends. She wore a pink knitted bed jacket, and she was watching them with expectant eyes. Her bed jacket was like a fancy cardigan, all fluffy, with pearl buttons. A pair of slippers were side by side on the floor next to the bed. Sid could just see the white gleam of a porcelain chamber pot underneath her bed.

Auntie Glad reached out and switched on an electric lamp, which threw her shadow up against the wall. "That smells good, Mary," she said.

Mum put the tray down on the bedside table, then leaned over and kissed her cheek. "We're just back from picking up Sidney. And here he is to meet you."

"The young jockey, eh?" said Auntie Glad.

"That's me," said Sid, moving closer.

Auntie Glad's face stretched into a wide, gap-toothed grin. She was tiny and olive-skinned, with dark spots on her plump, softly wrinkled cheeks.

Like a ripe apricot, Sid thought.

"Sid's always been mad on horses," said Mum. "He's wanted to be a jockey ever since he saw Bill Broughton ride a winner. He wanted to be just like him."

"Bill Broughton," murmured Auntie Glad. "Now there's a rider for you. One of the best." She nodded at Sid. "I always loved the horses," she confided. "And I always liked a little flutter before I married my Cedric. But he didn't approve of the races, Cedric didn't." She leaned forward. "Don't suppose you've got any tips for me?"

Mum burst out laughing. "Auntie Glad!" she said. "You're full of surprises!"

"Tips?" Sid was taken aback. "Racing tips?"

"Yes," said Auntie Glad. "I listen to the races on the wireless. And I listen to those blokes talking about the different horses, and their form. But you'll have inside knowledge."

Sid laughed. "Not really," he said. "I just moved down here. But I hear Manawa is a favourite for the Cup."

"Oh yes, I know that dear, but I never did like to back a favourite. I like an outsider. Not too far on the outside, mind. I don't like to throw good money away. I like to back a horse that's a good risk, but not a dead cert. That's my pick."

"I might ride in that race," said Sid.

"Might you?" Auntie Glad shifted herself so that she sat up straighter. "Which horse are you riding?"

"Well…" said Sid awkwardly. "It's supposed to be Manawa."

"Not really?" gasped Auntie Glad. She looked at Mum, her eyes wide. "You must be that proud," she said.

Mum smiled. "Of course I am. He's a very good rider. He'd be the youngest ever, if he got in. But they have to do the trials first."

"Of course," said Auntie Glad.

"Yes," said Sid. "You have to get picked. And I haven't even done anything with Manawa yet. I've only just arrived here."

And who knows if he'll even like me? he thought.

Auntie Glad's eyes glowed. "I wish I could come and watch."

"I don't know if they'd let you," said Mum. "But you could come to the Cup race."

"If I'm well enough, Mary," said Auntie Glad softly.

Sid glanced at his mum. She was smiling at Auntie Glad, but Sid felt it was a sad sort of smile.

"Of course you will be, Auntie Glad!" said Mum. "We're looking after you. You're doing fine. And you're putting on weight. The other day, when we had one of those Nurse Maude nurses come out here, do you remember? She said you were looking marvellous."

Auntie Glad smiled. "She was a nice girl," she said. "She didn't look old enough to be a nurse, but I suppose she had to be. She was wearing the uniform." She leaned towards Sid. "You know what they say," she said.

"No," said Sid. "What do they say?"

"They say you know you're getting old when all the policemen start looking young." Auntie Glad cackled with laughter.

"Oh," said Sid.

"Well, policemen started looking young to me, years ago," said Auntie Glad with a grin. "And now the nurses do, too."

Mum laughed too. "She was young, that Nurse Maude."

"Was her name Maude?" asked Sid.

"Oh, no, they're all called Nurse Maude nurses. It's after the lady who started it. They do nursing in the community. It's a wonderful thing." She smoothed Auntie Glad's top sheet, which was turned back over the top of the paisley eiderdown. "All right, Glad, are you ready for your cup of tea?"

"First, can you pass me my dressing gown? I told you I wouldn't need a chamber pot. I go outside to the thunder box, like everybody else."

Mum took a dressing gown down from a hook on the bedroom door. "Here you are," she said. "And put your slippers on. But just you remember, there's no shame in using one."

"And would you mind taking that food back to the table?" said Auntie Glad. She winked at Sid. "I'm getting up and having breakfast with the family. Young Sidney's arrival has perked me up no end."

***

When Auntie Glad joined them, she was wearing a long, dark green dress made of some sort of fabric that rustled as she moved, and a matching jacket.

"Very smart, Gladys," said Dad. "Off to Ascot, are we?"

Auntie Glad cupped a hand around her ear. "What's that, Arthur?" she asked.

"I said you're looking very smart," said Dad, in a louder voice. "Pretty flash, for the farm."

"You look lovely, Glad," said Mum.

"We've got a visitor," grinned Auntie Glad. "That's a good enough reason to dress up." She seated herself at the table. "You must be proud of this boy, Arthur."

Sid's gaze shot to his dad's face, trying to read his expression.

Dad's face rarely gave much away, but right now, a slow smile was spreading over his craggy features, and a deep pride seemed to shine out of him.

"Very proud, Gladys," said Dad. "Very proud. He's a credit to his family. He's got more determination than anyone. He'll make New Zealand sit up and take notice, one of these days. Show them how it's done. Eh, son?" He turned his face towards Sid, his warm affection curling up the corners of his mouth.

Sid gulped, feeling his face growing hot with embarrassment. His dream of becoming a famous jockey still felt very personal. He loved the excitement of winning, of course, and he was keen on making lots of money one day. But 'showing New Zealand' sounded very prideful. And pride went before a fall. Everyone knew that.

"You're embarrassing him, Arthur," said Mum.

"He's fine, Mary," said Dad. "He wants fame. And we want him to have it. He'll love it when it happens."

"How's Beryl doing?" Sid asked, to change the subject.

"Oh, she's doing very well. She loves Training College," said Mum. "She's a clever girl, our Beryl. She's top of her class in just about everything."

Bill, sitting next to Sid, tugged on his sleeve. "Her favourite subject is Nature Study," said Bill. "I told her that means she has to like our ferrets, because they're nature."

"And she said they're a bit too much nature," said Bruce. "She doesn't like them because they stink."

"'Nature' means like the nature table at school," Mum told the twins. "You know, with autumn leaves and seed pods and fossils. And empty birds' nests. It's science."

"And a fish tank," said Bruce. "Our class has a fish tank. And pet mice. They're on the nature table, in a cage."

"There you are," said Mum. "Mice are smelly enough for any classroom. You can't put a ferret on a nature table. It'd stink the whole room out."

They all laughed. Auntie Glad's cackle was loudest of all.

"Beryl doesn't like to boast," said Dad, "but she told me the head of the English department commended her for..." He looked at Mum. "What was it, Mary?"

"Creativity, attention to detail, and outstanding achievement."

"There you go," said Dad. "That's praise. Our Beryl is going to be a marvellous teacher."

"Things have turned out really well for Beryl," said Sid.

"She made a sacrifice and she's been rewarded," said Mum.

"Yes," said Sid softly. "I reckon she has."

He gazed around the table. The other person who was missing was Ruby.

Mum said, "We'll see Ruby in the holidays. She stays at school all term. I didn't like the idea at first, but now I think it's for the best."

"They've got all sorts of ways of getting them to learn to talk," said Dad. "They watch their breath moving bits of fabric. That's one thing. So they know how loud they're talking."

Mum sighed. "It must be very hard for them. At least Ruby could already talk a bit. But she's getting a proper education, that's what matters."

"They're not allowed to do sign language," said Bill. "But we saw them sneakily signing to each other. Didn't we, Bruce? When we first visited."

"Yeah," Bruce mumbled, his mouth full of toast.

"Ruby couldn't believe her eyes," said Mum. "Seeing those kids signing. But they stopped as soon as one of the teachers turned up."

***

Sid spent the next part of the day with Dad, who was keen to show him the farm.

"A little piece of paradise," he said.

Sid nodded. "It sure is." To his surprise, it already felt like home.

The twins showed Sid their cured rabbit skins, their tree hut, and the museum they'd created in a shed.

"It's even better than our old museum," said Bruce.

Their new museum had a huge goat's skull in pride of place. Sid picked it up, hefting its weight in his hand. It had massive, curling horns but was surprisingly light.

"We found that on the roof of the barn," said Bill. "It must have been there for ages. It was all bleached from the sun."

"But we bleached it a bit more," said Bruce. "With Mum's bleach."

"It looks very clean," said Sid.

Their museum also had the usual birds' nests, acorns and horse chestnuts, some perfect fossils of shells, chunks of petrified wood, and an impressive rock collection. Their collection even boasted a bit of greenstone.

Sid picked up the greenstone. It was an ordinary-looking grey oval stone, that sat heavily in the palm of his hand. But it had a slice cut off at one end, and inside, you could see translucent green.

"Wow," said Sid. "Did you cut it?"

"No," said Bruce. "I don't think we could cut rock. We got given it."

"By a man up the road," said Bill. "He collects rocks. He's even got gold."

"Yeah," said Bruce. "He's from way down south. He's got all his rocks in a glass cabinet. He showed them to Dad, and we were with him."

"And he gave us this one," said Bruce. "He said the South Island is where greenstone comes from. Pounamu, he called it."

"It's nowhere else," said Bruce. "Except China, and that's different. That's not greenstone, it's jade."

"And did you know the Māori word for the South Island is 'greenstone waters'?" asked Bill.

"No," said Sid.

"Te Wai Pounamu," Bill said carefully, working hard to pronounce it right.

From the house, a bell rang.

"Afternoon tea," yelled Bruce. He took the stone from Sid's hand and replaced it among the rocks of their collection, then the three boys raced each other back to the house.

***

They had afternoon tea sitting in the shade of an enormous old oak tree in the garden. There was a big pot of tea, and Mum had put out her best Royal Doulton tea set with the dainty cups and saucers and the square plates. Auntie Glad sat in a comfortable wicker chair with lots of cushions.

Mum frowned at Bill and Bruce, who were drinking tea with their little fingers crooked, and posh expressions on their faces. "Just be careful, you two. Woe betide you if you break one of my cups."

She had made sponge cake, with jam and whipped cream, yoyos, with vanilla icing squished between two melting layers of shortbread, and crumbly chocolate afghans, topped with a swirl of dark chocolate icing with half a walnut pressed into it.

"Our own eggs in the sponge," said Mum. "And our own walnuts on the afghans. There's a tree in the garden."

"Wow," said Sid. "An impressive spread, Mum."

"It's a bit fancy," admitted Mum. "But it's very special, having you home."

***

The drive back to Ridgeways seemed far too short. The car growled its way back up the steep driveway, then crunched along gravel roads through the Rangiora countryside. Sid rolled down his window and breathed in the soft country air. The wide paddocks on either side were golden with late afternoon light. Sid gazed dreamily out of the window until they reached the main road and sped towards Christchurch and Ridgeway racing stables.

Sid's heart sank as they approached the gates of Ridgeways. It was a hollow, unhappy feeling that seemed to spread right through him, radiating out from the pit of his stomach. The car stopped outside the main building and he climbed out, glancing left and right. There seemed to be nobody around. That was good.

Dad got out of the car too, and stretched his arms.

"Looks like they've packed up for the day," he said. He took off his hat. "Good luck, son. We'll see you again soon."

"Yup," said Sid. He waited for a moment, wondering if his dad was going to hug him, which he never, ever did.

Dad simply dipped his head in a slow nod of acknowledgement. "Good boy," he said. "You're doing well. Don't worry too much about Manawa – you'll know how to handle him. You've got what it takes."

"Thanks Dad," said Sid, his heart warmed by the unexpected praise.

He watched as his dad put his hat back on, climbed into the car and turned it in a wide circle, then drove out between the gates, heading for home. Sid turned away and trudged towards the bunk rooms. That sinking feeling in the pit of his stomach hadn't gone away. If anything, it felt worse. He wasn't looking forward to tomorrow.

Chapter Fifteen

Horses Are Healers

The next morning, Sid woke early in stuffy, semi-darkness. Waves of gentle snoring filled the bunk room. He peered down over the edge of his bunk. Below him, Sam was sleeping, his sunburned, freckled face peaceful in the half-light of dawn. Sid climbed quietly down from his bunk, pulled on his clothes, and slipped outside.

He breathed in deeply, filling his lungs with fresh morning air. Somewhere, an early bird twittered the first call of the day, and the wind whispered in the poplar trees behind the sleeping quarters. The dawn was a red glow on the horizon, and nobody else was about.

But lights were on over in the kitchen. Maybe he could get a cup of tea, like yesterday? Although it was probably way too early. He started off anyway, to try his luck, then stopped in his tracks as he spotted a slim figure stealthily leaving the cookhouse from a side door. A red coat glowed in the light from the doorway. It was Kiri.

Sid halted where he was. The girl didn't look in his direction. As before, she headed for the industrial area, moving fast, her footsteps silent on the grass. Her silhouette against the dawn light revealed the bump of a bulging bag. Questions pinged in Sid's brain.

Maybe she's feeding an animal?

He watched as Kiri's slight figure disappeared behind the bulky outline of the cookhouse.

Maybe she's hiding somebody?

What was that book they'd read at school? Kidnapped, by Robert Louis Stevenson. Scenes from the classic adventure story flashed through his mind. The Scots hiding from the English. Women risking their lives to bring them food...

Dummy, he told himself. This is New Zealand, and it's 1947. Not Scotland way back whenever.

And whatever Kiri was up to, it was none of his business. He wasn't nosy. Absolutely not. He was curious. Yes, curious, that much he could admit. It was a mystery.

He felt like following, but that would definitely be wrong.

I'm here to ride. To ride, and to win.

Ignoring the conflicting thoughts in his head, he allowed his feet to lead him to the canteen.

***

He opened the door and stepped inside. The room was warm. A clatter of dishes rattled on the other side of the servery hatch. He looked longingly at the wooden slats, as if staring at them would make them open.

Suddenly, they flew up, revealing the bulky figure of Mrs O'Brien.

"You again!" she said. "You're an early bird, that's for sure!"

"Good morning," said Sid. "I hope you don't mind."

"Of course not, love," she said. "Not at all. Want a cuppa? I've made a small pot just for the kitchen. I'll pour you one, if you like."

"Oh, thank you," said Sid. "Yes, I'd love that."

"Sugar?" she asked.

"One, please," said Sid.

He took the cup and saucer and sat at a table by the window, where he could watch the sun rise. The window was slightly open, and the fresh morning air drifted in, fragrant with the scent of cut hay. Magpies warbled in the distance, and in the nearby trees, hundreds of birds sang as the rim of the sun sprang up above the horizon, dazzling his eyes.

It reminded him of home. A wave of nostalgia engulfed him. Blinking hard, he stirred his tea, fighting to shake off the memories. Actually, he realised, the familiar dawn helped, in a strange sort of way. Some things were universal, he decided. The excitement of a new day was a good feeling, no matter where you were. He picked up his cup of tea.

The canteen door opened, and Sid froze, but it wasn't Carter or his mates. Mr Te Waka, the horse trainer, stepped inside. His eyes met Sid's across the room.

"Mōrena, young fellow," he said. "Up with the lark, eh?"

Sid grinned. "Yes," he said.

"Mind if I join you?" asked Mr T.

"Of course not," said Sid.

Mr Te Waka intrigued him. He watched as the trainer got himself a cup of tea, poured out by Mrs O'Brien. The cup rattled in the saucer as he carried it across to Sid's table.

"That's the ticket," said Mr T, seating himself opposite Sid. "Always start the day with a cup of tea." He took a sip, then set his cup down on the saucer and leaned back in his chair, gazing out of the window. "Beautiful," he said.

"Yup," said Sid. "Sure is."

Mr Te Waka studied him. "How did yesterday go, with your dad?"

"It was good," said Sid. "I saw my mum too, and my brothers. And an auntie I never knew I had."

"That can happen," said Mr T.

"And their new house," said Sid.

"New house?" asked Mr Te Waka.

"They moved here from the North Island," said Sid. "To Rangiora. I hadn't seen them for ages until they picked me up at the train station. They've got five acres," he added. "In a valley."

"So, you didn't want to move with them when they moved here?" asked Mr T.

"I'd already started my apprenticeship," said Sid. "So I stayed in Foxton, working for Mr Thorndon." Sid's stomach clenched as he said the name, his resentment flaring up. "Until he sent me here," he muttered.

Mr Te Waka raised an eyebrow, but said nothing. He turned his attention back to the view outside, where the sun was now well above the horizon. The chorus of birdsong coming in through the open window had reached its peak. "Best time of the day," he said. He finished his cup of tea and stood up, pushing back his chair. "Well," he said, "I'll be off. Come and see me, if you get a chance. You can meet young Stevie. He'll be spending the day with me."

***

After the early morning two-mile gallops, Sid and the other jockeys washed down their horses and turned them out to graze. Sid hurried through the rest of his morning tasks; mucking out and exercising horses. It was late morning by the time he was done.

It wouldn't hurt to go and see Mr T, he thought.

As soon as he could, he slipped away to the quiet paddock in front of Mr Te Waka's small recovery stable.

Filigree was munching hay out of a feed bag hanging from the wooden fence railing. She whinnied when she saw him. Beside her was a young, skinny kid with fair hair, cut very short. Two bulging sacks of hay lay on the ground near him. The boy looked up as Sid approached.

"Hello," said Sid. "Are you Stevie?"

The boy didn't answer.

Mr Te Waka came out of the stable, leading a sorrel gelding with a bandage around one foreleg. "Sidney!" he said. "Good timing. This is Findaway. The vet's just been and checked on him. He's doing nicely."

He led Findaway to the railing where another hay-stuffed feed bag was hanging.

Sid reached out his hand, palm up, and Findaway nuzzled into it.

Mr T laughed. "This horse has had a lot of treats lately. He expects them now." He smiled at Findaway. "Eat your hay. Hay is good for horses." The horse dipped his nose into the bag and pulled out a mouthful of hay.

Mr T glanced down at the fair-haired boy. "And this is Stevie."

Stevie stared at Sid, still not saying a word.

Sid studied him. The kid seemed like he was around eight or nine years old. He had startlingly blue eyes and patches of red, peeling skin on his nose and cheeks. His expression was odd, Sid thought. Sort of blank. Or guarded.

Mr T pulled a folded-up canvas hat from his pocket, shook it out, and handed it to Stevie. "Here you go, son," he said. "Put it on. No point in getting burnt."

The boy put the hat on his head, tugging it down. His expression didn't change.

"Good lad," said Mr T. "Come on then. Let's give them some hay, shall we?" He picked up one of the sacks of fresh hay and handed it to Stevie, then picked up the other and handed it to Sid.

Sid noticed the boy's expression brighten as he followed the trainer, his arms around the bulging sack. Wisps of hay drifted up into the air and wafted behind him as he marched along the fence-line, heading for a feed bag. Sid went in the opposite direction around the paddock, loading hay into feed bags hanging from wooden pegs. The horses grazing in the paddock made their way to the feed bags. They seemed to know which was theirs.

Mr Te Waka returned to the stable, leaving Stevie to finish feeding out the hay. Sid followed. He watched as Mr T untied Findaway and turned him out into the paddock with the other horses.

"A bit of supplement," said Mr Te Waka. "The hay. The grass is already drying up. It's going to be a hot summer."

Suddenly, a tall, lithe figure vaulted the fence, seeming to appear out of nowhere. Sid stared.

"Mōrena, Matt," said Mr T.

"Mōrena." The young man grinned, white teeth flashing in his dark face. "Want some help?"

"Of course," said Mr Te Waka. He glanced at Sid, then back at Matt. "Have you met Sid?"

"No," said Matt.

"This is Sidney Everett," said Mr T, "our newest jockey. And a real horseman."

Real horseman. Sid's heart lifted at these words.

"Sid," continued Mr Te Waka, "meet Matt. Ex-jockey, and now a very promising trainer."

Sid eyed Matt, feeling a little intimidated. He figured Matt was not much older than himself, but he already seemed like a man. He squared his shoulders and stood as tall as he could. "Good morning," he said.

"Good morning," said Matt. "Yeah, I got too heavy for the horses. Lucky I had the chance to help with the training. Now, it's all I do."

"A natural," said Mr T. "He's a natural. Well, come on, you two. We'll get Filigree doing some work and make a decision. I think she might be ready to race again."

Sid noticed that while they had been talking, young Stevie had finished stuffing the feed bags with hay and wandered off, leaving his empty sack on the ground. He was with one of the mares who was munching from a feed bag, talking to her softly. Sid couldn't hear what he was saying, but his voice sounded happy.

"He's forgotten about us, now," said Mr Te Waka. "He'll be fine. Best thing for him, just hanging around with the horses."

He called out to him. "Stevie!"

The boy looked up.

"Bring the empty sack when you come back in."

The boy nodded.

Mr T turned to Sid. "I don't mind what he does while he's here, as long as he's grabbing hold of all the healing these horses can give him."

"Healing?" asked Sid.

"Horses are healers," said Mr Te Waka, taking Sid's empty sack. He shook it out and folded it. "They won't hurt you unless they've been mistreated or they're frightened. The horses I'm working with here are safe to be around. And Stevie is just soaking up all that peace and calm that horses naturally have."

Matt nodded. "The kid's had a hard time, and just being around horses is helping him."

Sid said, "When I was at home, if I ever had a bad day, I used to just go out and see my horse, Hugh. Just stand there with him in the paddock…" He gulped. His emotions always got stirred up at the memory of Hugh.

Mr T smiled an understanding smile. "That's exactly what we're talking about. Just being around horses can do wonders. It would do wonders for somebody else, eh Matt, if we could get him here?"

Matt flashed a quick glance at Sid, then looked back at Mr Te Waka with a frown. "Yeah, well. You can't force anything."

"I know," said Mr T. He looked at Sid. "Shouldn't you be heading off to lunch? I'm sure you've been working hard. You don't want to miss out."

Sid blinked. "Yes. Sure. I'll see you later."

He climbed back over the fence, puzzling about the snatch of conversation he'd just heard. The mention of somebody else who could do with some horse therapy. They obviously didn't want to tell him who it was. Another mystery.

A sudden hot gust of wind buffeted him as he made his way back to the canteen. The day was changing. While he'd been talking to Mr Te Waka, the soft, clear blue of the sky had changed to a menacing copper. A hot wind blew again, a stronger gust this time. He hurried into the cookhouse, glad to get into some shade.

Chapter Sixteen

A Dangerous Wind

In the canteen, Sid grabbed a tray. Lunch was shepherds' pie again. It looked good. He spotted Sam over on the far side of the room and went to join him.

"Good morning, mate," said Sam. "Weather's changing."

"It's a strong wind," agreed Sid.

"It's the nor'wester," said Sam. "That wind's a killer. It spooks the horses. You can't do anything with them when the nor'wester's blowing."

From the canteen window, Sid watched the sky as he ate. The burnished copper tint was muddier, and the branches of the trees were tossing about.

"Doesn't look good," he agreed. He stirred his tea and took a big gulp.

Glancing outside again, he spotted Kiri.

What...?

She walked with determination, like someone on a mission, head down against the wind. Her hair streamed out from under her cloth cap, whipping around in the rising wind. Once again, she was carrying a bulging bag.

"What's she up to?" he asked.

Sam glanced out of the window. "Kiri?"

"Yes," said Sid. "Is she going to the industrial area?"

Sam raised his eyebrows. "Dunno."

Sid remembered that he'd planned to keep quiet about his speculations. "I thought I saw her going there one other time, that's all," he said.

Sam shrugged. "She's not a jockey. She can do what she likes."

Sid frowned. He didn't mention the bag Kiri was carrying. Maybe it was just a picnic? It was none of his business; he told himself. And he didn't want to get her into trouble if she was up to something she shouldn't be. He understood that sometimes people had a good reason for not letting everyone know what they were doing.

But he was curious. He really wanted to find out what was going on.

No, he told himself. Focus on the riding. That's why you're here. It'll be worth it in the end, when you're famous.

"And rich," he said aloud.

"What?" asked Sam.

"Oh, nothing." Sid felt his face flush. "Just thinking." He sat up straight and looked around the room, feeling suddenly stifled. He could do with some fresh air. Carter was just coming in the door, and that made it a good time to leave. He stood up, pushing his chair back.

"Thinking?" Sam grinned up at him. "Too much thinking's bad for the brain. Wears it out."

Sid laughed. "Is that what they teach you, down here in the South Island?"

"Mainland," corrected Sam. "This is the Mainland. You lot are on the Ika of Maui. The fish Maui pulled up out of the sea."

"Oh, right. Well, it's pretty nice up there. For a fish." Sid pushed his chair back under the table. "I'm off," he said. "See you later."

"Where are you going?" asked Sam.

"Just getting some fresh air," said Sid.

***

Sid tracked Kiri from a distance. He knew he was being nosy. Nevertheless, he kept going. Ahead was the stand of Kahikatea trees. They were tall, creepy old trees, so solid they barely moved in the wind.

Kiri disappeared amongst the towering trunks, slipping out of sight like a shadow. Sid hurried across the grass, squinting his eyes against the wind, his ears full of its roaring. A powder-coating of dust and wind-blown grit peppered his cheeks. His feet slipped on the dry grass, and dust coated his tongue as soon as he opened his mouth. He stumbled on until he reached the edge of the stand of trees.

Stepping into the bush, he felt relieved at the sudden stillness, his feet secure on the forest path. The gale roared in the treetops, but it couldn't reach him at ground level. Dappled light and shadow flickered down from high above, where the upper branches tossed and swayed.

It was another world. The spicy, mysterious fragrance of kahikatea filled his nostrils, making his heart leap. It didn't smell quite the same as the bush back home.

Kahikatea trees have their own smell, he decided.

A flash of red in the distance ahead warned him he'd better hurry to catch up. He wouldn't know which way to go if Kiri turned off the main path. Determined to find out what was going on, he increased his pace, almost running along the track. He just hoped she wouldn't be mad at him.

Suddenly, a figure leaped out of the bushes.

Kiri stood barring the path, hands on hips, her face a scowl of anger. "What do you think you're playing at?" she snarled.

Chapter Seventeen

Caught Out

S id reeled back.

How did she do that?

"You reckon you can sneak up on me? Think again, mate." Kiri's face flushed with anger. "This isn't 'Cowboys and Indians'. Didn't you get enough of that at school?"

Stung, Sid blinked at her. "I wasn't playing a game. I was just curious, that's all."

"Nosy, more like," she said.

"I thought you might need some help," said Sid. He knew it sounded lame as soon as the words left his lips.

Help? Nah. She was right. He had to admit it; he was being nosy.

"Help?" She raised scornful eyebrows. "I don't need any help, Sid from Foxton. I'm quite able to do what I want, when I want, without any help from you." She lifted her chin, her dark eyes burning. "Go back."

"But..." Sid didn't want to go back.

Kiri glared. "I said go back! You can't do anything to help. And I don't need your help." She curled her lip. "If that's actually what you wanted."

Sid winced. He felt like a ten-year-old, caught stealing a biscuit. The wind gave a sudden extra-hard gust, and the tree tops high above creaked and groaned. "I don't know how safe it is to be here," he said. "There's some kind of storm brewing."

Kiri hadn't finished. She lowered her voice. "This is something you don't need to know about. You might even make things worse." Then she sighed, and her shoulders relaxed a little. "I suppose you didn't mean any harm. But curiosity killed the cat. Don't you know that? There's serious stuff happening here, and the less you know about it, the better." Her lips quivered. "You can't help. Nobody can help." She took a deep breath and squared her shoulders. "So go back. Now."

She glanced into the bushes beside the path. Her bag lay there, a loaf of bread spilling out onto the leaf litter of the forest floor.

"Now look what you made me do," she said. "Uncle Dan's bread." She clapped her hand over her mouth.

Sid looked at the bag and the spilled bread, then at Kiri. "Uncle Dan," said Sid triumphantly. "You're taking food to your uncle?"

"No." Kiri snatched the bag from the bushes and picked up the bread, dusting off some tiny, dry kahikatea leaves from its golden crust. "Nosy, like I said," she snapped.

"I'm not nosy. I just notice things, that's all." Sid tried to make his voice sound mature and reasonable.

"I told you," she said. "I can't talk about it. And you'd better forget what I said."

"Fine, then." Sid scowled. "I'm not interested in your uncle Dan, anyway. Whatever he's up to." A sudden idea struck him. "He's not an escaped convict, is he?"

Kiri burst out laughing. "No, he's not an escaped convict. What do you think this is? A hundred years ago?" She smiled at him. "Sorry I was mad at you," she said gruffly. "I could probably trust you." She eyed him thoughtfully, then shook her head. "But nah, best not. You might blab."

"I'd never blab." Sid was stung. "I'm very good at keeping secrets. I've often had to, in the past."

She grinned. "I won't ask what sort of secrets."

"Dumb ones, as it turned out," admitted Sid.

"I have to keep moving." Kiri suddenly looked worried. "I haven't got much time. I'm starting work again soon, to prep for dinner. Go back, Sid. And don't follow me again."

Sid stared at her, his heart sinking. "Really?"

"Really," said Kiri firmly.

He lingered stubbornly on the path.

"Go on. Get!" she said.

In the gaping mouth of the bag, Sid glimpsed a tartan blanket and a tin of something.

"No harm done," Kiri muttered. She stuffed the loaf back into her bag and slung it over her shoulder. "Bye, Sid."

Turning abruptly, she hurried away along the track, leaving Sid standing alone. A bend in the path hid her from view. It was like she'd never been there.

Okay, so that's what's going on.

Sid hesitated. Actually, he still didn't know what was going on, but he knew when he wasn't wanted. He gave one last, lingering look along the track, then turned and retraced his steps.

She probably thinks I'm an idiot. He trudged reluctantly back along the track. Back to Ridgeways. Back to feeling like an outsider.

She doesn't want my help. She thinks I'm nosy. Anger flared up inside him. Rejection was always a bitter pill to swallow. Sid told himself that he didn't care. That Kiri and her mystery were of no interest to him.

I'm here for the horse racing. I'm going to be rich and famous. And that's all that matters.

He sensed he was nearing the edge of the small forest. The treetops high above him groaned and tossed in the wind that roared across the land. He stepped out into its full blast.

Chapter Eighteen

The Nor'wester

The nor'wester hit him full in the face as he left the shelter of the kahikatea trees. It roared in his ears, buffeting him so that he stumbled sideways. He staggered forward across the grass, squinting his eyes against the dust.

Sam was standing near the stable, sheltering from the wind, one hand shielding his eyes from the dust and the glare. He waved when he spotted Sid.

"Where have you been, mate?" he shouted.

Sid jogged over to him.

"Nowhere," he said. "What's going on?"

Sam gave him a puzzled look. "We're waiting for an announcement. Everyone's been told to wait in the canteen. Come and get yourself another cup of tea. You look like you need one."

They crossed the lawn, leaning into the wind, and flung open the door. It slammed behind them as they lurched into the room.

The quiet inside almost made Sid's ears ring after the roar of the wind outside. Everyone was there, sitting in absolute silence. Not one person spoke.

Sid got himself a cup of tea, trying to make as little noise as possible. He added some sugar and joined Sam at the table. He noticed the kitchen staff busy about their tasks. They could use Kiri's help. Did they know where she was?

He remembered the newspaper ad in the personal column. He was pretty sure that Mrs O'Brien knew what Kiri was up to. Perhaps they all knew. Maybe everyone here knew about 'Uncle Dan' except for him. He wanted to ask Sam about it, but then he'd be giving away a secret. Unless Sam already knew? He glanced at his friend's honest, freckled face. No. That face couldn't hide any secrets, he was pretty sure. He picked Sam as the sort of person who couldn't hide a secret to save his life.

The door banged open. Mr MacDonald entered, and with him was Mr Ridgeway, the owner. That meant it was serious.

Sid had a sudden fear that something had happened to Kiri, over in the industrial area. He pushed the thought aside. This meeting was about the nor'wester. Nothing to do with Kiri. And she could take care of herself. She'd made that clear.

***

"Attention, everyone," said Mr MacDonald.

The room was still.

"We're cancelling all outside work, as you will have guessed. No morning gallops. No training whatsoever. It's impossible, and dangerous, to work with the horses in this wind. It can be a killer. Don't spend time outside if you can help it."

He scanned the room, his gaze seeming to linger on Sid's face.

"Close all doors and windows and keep them shut. Latch gates securely. Double check any gates whenever you open and close them. Keep a close eye on the horses and on their water. Look to their safety, and to the safety of every person here."

He cleared his throat. "Now, Mr Ridgeway would like a word."

Mr Ridgeway stepped forward and waited a moment. Sid could hear the wind growling around outside, like some gigantic animal trying to get in. The timber of the wooden-framed building shuddered at every fierce blast. The corrugated iron roof rattled and banged somewhere overhead where it wasn't securely fastened down.

Looking around him, Sid saw that every face was pinched and serious. All eyes watched Mr Ridgeway, waiting for him to speak. Mr Ridgeway was slow in his movements, but he exuded an unmistakable air of intelligence and power.

He's like a general, Sid thought. Commanding his troops.

"Thank you, everyone, for your patience," said Mr Ridgeway. "We've made the only decision possible. We obviously can't work with the horses under these conditions. Hopefully, the wind will have blown itself out by the time the trials are scheduled. The dates for the Cup are set in stone, so we'll have to work twice as hard once the wind drops."

He raked the room with his steely gaze.

"Now," he continued. "You all know that this is a dangerous wind. Our primary concern is with the horses. It drives them crazy. We'll be checking on them regularly, making sure they're coping."

He glanced at a piece of paper in his hand. "While we wait, we'll be doing a bit of tidying up, and a bit of extra grooming. I've got a list here. We'll polish anything that needs polishing. You can clean your gear. Mend your silks. Darn your socks."

A polite chuckle ran around the room, then faded into silence. Outside, the wind roared, but in the canteen, you could have heard a pin drop.

"We'll check over the saddles," Mr Ridgeway continued. "And all the harnesses. Sort out anything that needs repairing. Send anything away that needs re-stitching, and oil the leather. Everything in the tack room could do with a once-over. We'll feed out as much as we have to. Then we'll just sit out the storm. It's all we can do."

Sid glanced sideways at Sam. Sam was nodding, agreeing with everything.

Mr Ridgeway continued. "Look after yourselves. Stay indoors as much as possible. And drink plenty of water. Dehydration's a real danger in this weather. And that goes for the horses, too. We need to make sure they have plenty of water at all times."

He gazed around the room. "Any questions?"

Nobody said anything.

He turned to Mr MacDonald. "All yours," he murmured.

He went to the door and opened it. The wind caught it, whipping it out of his hand and banging it against the wall of the building. Mr Ridgeway turned and surveyed the room. "And that's just a small taste of what's coming," he said. He disappeared outside, carefully closing the door behind him.

***

Mr MacDonald's eyes gleamed as he turned back to the silent crowd. "Right. You heard the boss. Let's get on with the new plan, and hope the wind dies down soon." He looked at Sid. "Everett?"

"Yes, Mr MacDonald?" Sid kept his voice steady, and he remained sitting down. He felt everyone staring at him, but his eyes didn't leave MacDonald's.

"Never been in a nor'wester before, I don't suppose?"

"No, sir," said Sid.

"I hope you've got what it takes. They breed them tough, down here. Not sure about where you're from."

Sid waited.

"It's true grit that counts here, in this sort of weather," Mr Mac-Donald said.

Sid resisted the urge to roll his eyes.

What's his problem? Why does he always have to have a go? He kept his face impassive, ignoring the fact that everyone's eyes were turned on him like searchlights.

MacDonald glared, waiting for a response, but Sid didn't answer. Instead, he kept his gaze steady, his expression unflinching. Finally, Mr MacDonald looked away. He cast a baleful glare around the room. "All right," he barked. "That's it. As you were." He turned on his heel and headed for the door.

As it closed after him, a buzz of conversation broke out, filling the room.

Sid let out a long sigh of relief.

Sam leaned over. "Ignore him," he said.

"How can I ignore him," said Sid, "when he singles me out like that, in front of everybody?"

Sam shrugged. "I don't understand it. He's really out to get you."

"The thing is," said Sid, "it's all not true."

"What's not true?"

"That my dad is friends with the boss."

"Not to worry," said Sam. "If they're smart, everyone will see it doesn't tie up with the sort of person you are."

Sid changed the subject. "So, what happens with this wind? I suppose we'll be busy?"

"Nah," said Sam. "There won't be a lot of work. At first there'll be a bit, with the cleaning and mending. Then they'll get out the dart boards and the packs of cards. There's not much here that needs mending. Most of the gear's in good nick. You wait and see." He grinned. "I hope you play a good game of poker."

Sid squirmed. He'd never played poker. 'Last Card' was the game they played at home. And at school they'd played Five Hundred, secretly. The teachers confiscated any cards found at school and sent a note home to the parents.

But he had a feeling that he wouldn't be playing too many games of cards. Or darts. He suspected that Mr MacDonald would make sure he had plenty of work to keep him occupied. And he was pretty sure he would find him the worst jobs he possibly could.

Chapter Nineteen

Work

For three long days, Mr MacDonald kept Sid hard at work. Each day, he seemed to be on his own, mucking out, feeding out, cleaning, and scrubbing.

On day three, Sam managed to join him.

He looked around the stable, and at Sid, working alone. "You seem to have your work cut out," he said.

"You reckon?" said Sid. He paused in mucking out a stall, lifting a pitchfork full of hay and horse manure. He dumped it into a wheelbarrow and wiped his brow with the back of one arm.

"You know they've got a tournament on?" asked Sam.

"What sort of tournament?" said Sid.

"Oh, you know," said Sam. He seemed to regret mentioning it. "Darts. I'm not in it." He dug into his pocket. "I've got something for you, mate," he said, and pulled out a lumpy parcel wrapped in a linen napkin. "Here you go." He held it out.

Sid stared at it.

"It's fruitcake," said Sam. "It tastes just like Christmas cake, only better. It's from Mrs O'Brien."

Sid took the parcel and unwrapped it, welling up with emotion at the unexpected kindness. It was an enormous slab of cake, cut into several slices.

"Thank her very much for me," he said. He sat down on the hay-strewn floor of the stable, leaning his back against the nearest stall. "She's very kind, that Mrs O'Brien," he muttered. He looked up at Sam. "Do you want a piece?" he asked.

Sam shook his head. "I'm alright," he said.

A horse's head leaned down, nudging Sid's shoulder. It was Manawa.

"At least I've got to know Manawa," he said. He grinned and broke off a piece of cake, holding it out on the palm of his hand, and waited as the horse gently gathered it up with his lips.

"I hope cake is good for horses," said Sam.

"Bound to be," said Sid. "All that fruit. Gotta be good for them."

"Yeah," agreed Sam.

Sid started munching. "This is perfect fruitcake," he mumbled, his mouth full.

Sam gazed around. "All this work, all by yourself," he said. "It's not fair. Old MacDonald's making you work harder than anyone else. And with no company."

"My own company's better, sometimes," said Sid. "Not better than your company, though," he added. "I wish he'd put us together. It might actually be fun. And we'd get it done twice as fast."

"I can't understand why he's got it in for you," said Sam.

"It's all about the Cup. He wants Carter to ride Manawa," said Sid.

"Isn't that up to Mr Ridgeway?" asked Sam. "MacDonald can make recommendations, but Mr Ridgeway makes the final decision."

"It's more like it's up to Manawa," said Sid. "He hates everybody except for Wade Daker, and he's in hospital. So, this is working to my advantage. Manawa doesn't mind me. He might even like me. Eh, boy?" He looked up at the gleaming black stallion's head, hovering over his own.

The horse whickered softly.

Sam whistled. "You might be right," he said.

"Don't worry about me, Sam. Things are working out just fine," said Sid. "And thanks for the cake!" He wrapped the uneaten pieces of cake back up in the linen napkin, and placed the small parcel up high on a shelf. "For later," he said.

Sam nodded. "Okay, I'm off," he said.

"Thank Mrs O'Brien for me," said Sid.

"I will." Sam opened the stable door. The wind howled in, making the loose hay swirl around in small tornadoes. He stepped outside, and the door slammed shut behind him.

Sid went to the window and watched until Sam disappeared in the haze of wind-blown dust. Then he picked up the pitchfork. At least all this work was building up his muscles.

Pausing by Manawa's stall, he looked up at the huge black horse. Manawa snorted and dipped his head, nuzzling Sid's ear.

"We're friends now, aren't we?" he asked the horse. "Best mates. We'll win that race, won't we?"

Manawa snorted and stamped.

"I'll take that as a 'yes'," said Sid, scooping up another pitchforkful of hay.

***

That night, Sid couldn't sleep. The wind roared outside; the rafters creaked and groaned, and a sheet of roofing iron that was coming loose was banging up and down above his head. That, and the snores of the other jockeys filling the air inside the bunk room, made sleep impossible.

This is ridiculous, Sid thought. I'm exhausted. I need to sleep.

He knew what the problem was. The anxiety about the coming trials, whenever they might be, was making his stomach twist itself into knots.

Finally, he could stand it no longer. Moving carefully, he lowered his pillow over the side of his bunk to the floor, followed by one of his grey, woollen blankets. Then he climbed down, gathered up his clothes for the morning and tiptoed across the floor.

Not that any of them are likely to hear me, he thought.

He opened the door, hanging on tight as the wind tried to snatch it from his hands. Gritting his teeth, he closed it securely, fighting the wind, which tried to slam it shut. Then, with one arm over his face to protect himself from the stinging grains of dust, he found his way to the stable. He groped for the latch, and let himself in.

Once secure inside the stable, Sid waited for a moment, letting his eyes adjust to the gloom. He listened to the familiar sounds of horses breathing and shifting their feet. The soft, hay-scented dimness felt like an old friend welcoming him. As his eyes adjusted, he could make out the form of the grey mare next to the door. He reached out a hand and stroked her nose, and she whickered a welcome. In the gloom beyond, another horse snorted.

Although it was dark, Sid could sense all the horses, alert in their stalls. Clutching his blanket and pillow, he crept along, counting the stalls until he reached Manawa. He banged his shin on something that gave a loud clang, and a sharp pain shot up his leg. Reaching down, his hand found a curved metal rim, and he dipped his fingers into cool liquid. A full bucket of water stood in his way.

A horse snorted in the gloom next to him.

"Manawa? Is that you?" He reached up into the warm darkness and felt the velvet touch of an enquiring nose. Manawa nuzzled the palm of his hand.

"I didn't bring any apple, sorry. Or any cake."

He felt Manawa's head lift away from his hand, and then a whiskery chin brushed against his cheek. He smiled. "But we're friends anyway, aren't we?"

Sid bundled up his pillow and blanket, tucking them under his arm.

"I'm dossing down with you tonight," he said. "Move over, big boy."

He climbed over into the stall, ignoring the pain in his shin, and made a bed of hay in the corner. Wrapping his blanket around himself, he pummelled his pillow into shape, then snuggled down.

The world outside was full of the roaring of the wind. But in the warm stable, Sid relaxed. He could hear the soft sound of horses breathing, and smell the sweet, dry fragrance of hay. Sid sensed Manawa standing near him, and smiled as he breathed in the soothing, horsey smell. Up high was the rectangular shape of a window. The darkness outside seemed slightly less dense. Was that a star? Did that mean that the wind was dropping?

He closed his eyes, trying to focus on his own breathing, listening to the horses' gentle sounds, willing his thoughts to stop their whirling. That whirling which seemed to perfectly match the whirling of the hot, dusty wind outside.

Chapter Twenty

Manawa

Morning light was streaming in through the dusty rectangle of the stable window. Sid awoke to the tickle of Manawa nuzzling him and a snort resounding in his ear. He opened his eyes to see Manawa's long, black whiskers trailing across his face like a big, friendly spider.

He laughed. "Good morning," he said, gazing up at the massive, dark head inches from his nose.

Manawa snorted again, blowing warm, hay-scented breath into his face.

Sid scrambled to his feet. "I slept a lot better in a stall with you than with the humans over in the bunk room," he said. He put his forehead to Manawa's nose. "How about you? Did you sleep okay with an intruder in the corner?"

Manawa dipped his head.

"I'll take that as a 'yes.'" Sid stroked the glossy black neck, and Manawa whickered a greeting. High above him, the wind whistled through the rafters of the building. The other horses in the stable eyed him curiously, ears pricked as if waiting to find out what he was going to do.

"I'm going to have breakfast," he told them.

He tucked his blanket and pillow out of sight in a dark corner and tugged on his clothes, then slipped out of Manawa's stall. The bucket of water on the floor had a thick film of dust lying on the surface. The nor'wester left its mark everywhere, sifting dust onto everything.

Sid walked quietly between the rows of horses, feeling their eyes watching him as he went. As he neared the door, the roar of the wind became louder. It whistled through the cracks between the boards and around the door and almost shook the building.

He grasped the handle and opened the door, holding tight so that the wind didn't snatch it out of his hand, then closed it securely and hurried over to the cookhouse. The wind shrieked in his ears, and his cheeks stung with flying dust as he crossed the withered grass that had been a lawn. The windows of the cookhouse glowed in the distance.

The canteen was the usual warm haven, fragrant with the smell of toast. This time, he would not linger. He'd grab some breakfast and take it back to the stable.

"Good morning, Sidney," said Mrs O'Brien. "An early bird, as always."

"Good morning," said Sid.

He poured himself a cup of strong tea, added sugar, and buttered an enormous pile of toast. The wind outside was too strong to risk using a plate. He stuck his slices of toast face to face, butter and marmite sticking together, piled them up, and wrapped them in a flour bag Mrs O'Brien gave him. She didn't ask questions.

He spotted a bowl of apples on a bench inside the kitchen.

"Mrs O'Brien? Can I have an apple?" he asked.

Mrs O'Brien gave him two; a large green apple and a small red one. He stuffed one in each pocket and downed his cup of tea.

Outside, Sid headed back to the stables, head down against the wind. He struggled with the latch on the stable door, holding the bag of toast between his teeth. Finally, he got the door open and slipped inside, relieved to hear the roar of the wind fade, as the door clicked shut.

Sid padded back along the row of stalls, enjoying the peace of horses at rest. There was the occasional stamp of a hoof. A soft whinny greeted him as he passed Lady Kate. Her ears were pricked up, and her eyes were bright with expectation.

"Hello, Lady Kate," he said. "Good morning." He stroked her soft nose. She nudged his shoulder.

A rustle in the hay at his feet startled him, and he looked down to see the grey flicker of a tiny, fast-moving mouse.

"Hey, mouse. I won't hurt you," he murmured, as the mouse disappeared from sight.

He gave Lady Kate the small red apple and continued along the walkway, his eyes fixed on Manawa.

"I'm back," he said.

A loud snort escaped the nostrils of the huge black horse as he approached. Manawa stood like an obsidian statue, his eye on Sid.

"Apple?" Sid asked. He pulled a large, green-skinned Granny Smith apple out of his pocket.

Manawa snorted again. Sid was pretty sure he liked apples.

"I'll have to cut it for you," he said. "It'd be a bit of a mouthful, even for a big boy like you."

He dug into his back pocket and pulled out Mr Thorndon's knife. With his thumbnail, he prised out the blade. He cut the apple. The sharp aroma wafted up, and he noticed Manawa's nostrils twitch in anticipation. He held out the cut piece on his open palm. Manawa dipped his head, and Sid felt the soft touch of the horse's lips as he delicately collected the piece of apple and ate it.

"More?" Sid cut another chunk, and Manawa again nuzzled his palm, gently taking the apple.

Sid eyed the giant horse. "You think we could go for a ride? When the wind stops, of course."

The horse regarded him solemnly, his dark eye gleaming. He tossed his mane and snorted again, stamping his foot in his stall.

"Easy, boy!" Sid smiled. "I know you're keen. Well, I hope you're keen. I hope you're not telling me you don't like anybody who comes from the Fish of Maui."

Manawa shook his head and stared at the apple.

"More apple?" Sid cut him another piece and held it out. As the horse took it, Sit reached up a hand and stroked the side of his neck. He kept on talking as he stroked, then moved his hand up to the horse's forelock to give it a scratch.

"There you go. Gotta stretch up high, don't I? You're such a tall fellow."

Manawa lowered his head and put his face close to Sid's.

Sid held his breath. Was this the fearsome Manawa who had everyone terrified? He rested his cheek against the horse's head, smelling his sweet, apple-scented breath, and slipped his free arm around the massive black neck.

"There you go, you beauty. You're a fine horse. A stunner. A winner." Sid lifted his face away and looked up into Manawa's dark eye, with its long lashes. "We'll show them, won't we? Together. You and me."

Sid cut more apple, noting that the horse appreciated each piece, and also that he had good manners. That was important, in a horse.

It was a sign of good training. He didn't see any reason why he should have trouble with this horse. What was all the fuss about?

Manawa munched the last of the apple. Sid wiped the blade of the knife on his trousers, closed it with a satisfying snap, and slipped it back into his pocket. Then he leaned his face once more against the horse's glossy neck.

Manawa lifted his head. He had heard something over the constant roar of the wind outside.

The door burst open, and a group of boys entered, talking loudly.

Chapter Twenty-One

Smoke

One of the boys banged the door shut again. "At least it's somewhere out of the wind," he said.

"Yeah, it's the best place to be. We can have a bit of a..." The boy broke off, spotting Sid.

"Well, what do you know? It's the wee lad from up north. Young... what's his name? Everett. Yeah." It was Tyler, one of Carter's cronies.

Sid straightened up, instantly watchful. He scanned the bunch. Tyler with the smirk, who always oiled his hair. And Fred Walters with a bleached thatch that was almost white. And Carter. Of course.

Tyler took a tin of tobacco and some cigarette papers from a pocket in his jacket.

"What are you doing?" asked Sid.

"What does it look like? Just rolling a smoke out of the wind." Tyler's lips tightened.

Sid glared at him. "You know you can't smoke in here."

"Oooh, listen to him," said Carter.

"Nah, he's right," said Fred Walters. His cheeks flushed red as he spoke. "It's a fire risk, in here."

Carter gave him a scornful glance, and Fred shut his mouth, his cheeks flushing an even deeper red.

Tyler rolled himself a thin cigarette, put it between his lips, and stuffed the tobacco and papers back in his pocket. Then he took out a box of matches.

"You can't light that in here," said Sid. "This place could go up in a flash."

Tyler's tight-lipped smirk twitched up higher at one corner, giving his face a lop-sided look. "Gonna stop me?"

He struck the match and held it to his cigarette. The end glowed as he inhaled. He watched Sid through half-closed eyes as he held out the still-burning match. "Ooooh, the match is burning down! I might have to drop it..."

The horses nearby were jostling anxiously, disturbed by the noise, their nostrils flaring in alarm at the smell of smoke.

Sid started towards him, rage exploding in his chest.

Tyler raised the match to his lips and blew it out. "As if I would," he said. "Got you going, though." He flicked the blackened remains of the match at Sid.

The match fell to the floor. Sid snatched it up and dropped it into the bucket of water, stamping his foot on the spot where the match had hit the floor, just to be sure. As he did so, Carter stretched out his foot, slipping it between Sid's ankles and hooking one of his legs out from under him.

Sid lurched sideways, banging his head against the nearest stall. He staggered, then regained his balance, and spun around to face Carter. "All right, Carter," he said.

"I've been looking forward to this, Everett," murmured Carter. "Gonna enjoy mashing your face into the floor."

"Just try it," Sid muttered between clenched teeth.

The two boys circled each other in the narrow space, fists raised, eyes locked on each other, watching for an opening. Sid's thoughts whirled as his feet moved carefully, his fists never dropping their guard.

Carter was older, and he was tough and wiry. But Sid was so fired up with fury at Tyler's recklessness that he felt invincible. Anyone who would willingly endanger horses shouldn't be working with horses. And anyone who supported that behaviour deserved a punch. Several punches.

Sid saw his chance. Feinting with his left, he landed a solid punch with his right on Carter's jaw, sending him reeling backwards. Carter staggered and crashed against the wooden wall of the empty stall opposite. Swearing, he pushed himself off the wall, and moved towards Sid, his eyes full of fury.

The other boys yelled encouragement as Carter came back swinging his fists, cheeks flushed and eyes glittering.

"I'll make you sorry for that, you little rat," he said.

He swung at Sid, catching him on the shoulder and knocking him back against the stall behind.

Sid pushed himself upright, a grunt escaping his lips, and launched straight back into the attack, landing a punch right in Carter's solar plexus. Carter staggered back, gasping.

Sid gathered himself for another attack, but before he could make his move, Carter rushed at him, grabbing him in a headlock. Sid broke free, turning his whole body, twisting Carter and tripping him with a foot between his legs as he spun. Carter grabbed hold of Sid as he crashed down, and then the two boys were on the ground, rolling and punching in the hay, the others yelling and cheering them on.

Sid tasted blood in his mouth. He sensed Carter was trying to pin him against the wall and struggled to keep the fight in the open walkway. He knew Carter was stronger, and that he'd have to win fast, or he wouldn't win at all. Pushing Carter back, his head ringing from a heavy blow, he squinted through eyes that didn't want to open properly.

He made a fist, and smacked Carter in the mouth, hearing the crunch and the yell of pain from his opponent. Making the most of the moment, he pulled himself out of Carter's grip, jumping on top of him and straddling his chest, trying to pin his arms down.

There was a sudden silence from the onlookers as a gust of wind whirled through the stable. Sid kept trying to fend off Carter's blows, struggling to pin him down, until muscular arms grabbed him, and jerked him to his feet.

Mr Ridgeway shook him, his face contorted, spitting out words Sid could hardly understand. But he understood enough to know that Mr Ridgeway was angry. Mr Ridgeway shook him again. "What the devil do you think you're playing at?" He glared at them. "My top jockeys, brawling in a stable. What's it all about?" He released his grasp, and Sid staggered, his head ringing.

Mr Ridgeway jerked Carter to his feet. "And what do you think you're doing? You've been here long enough to know better."

Mr Ridgeway was about to say something more, then he sniffed the air. "I smell smoke," he said.

Chapter Twenty-Two

Trouble

They all looked at Tyler.

Tyler looked at the bucket of water. His cigarette butt floated on the dusty surface, next to the dead match. He flicked a frightened glance at Mr Ridgeway and shrank back against one of the stalls. The horse behind him leaned over and sniffed at his pomaded hair.

"Tyler?" said Mr Ridgeway. "Were you smoking in here?"

Tyler tightened his lips and didn't reply.

"Not talking, eh?" Mr Ridgeway turned to Carter. "Let's have it."

Carter, his lips swelling up, stammered, "I...I..." He lapsed into silence.

Mr Ridgeway eyed the other member of Carter's gang. "Walters?"

Walters didn't answer either.

Mr Ridgeway looked at Sid. "Sidney Everett. Would you kindly tell me what has been going on in here?"

Sid knew he had to keep silent. He couldn't dob anyone else in, even though they deserved it.

Mr Ridgeway waited. Nobody spoke.

"All right," said Mr Ridgeway. "You've all had a chance to tell me. Now, you're all fired. Every single one of you. I don't care who you are, or which horse you're supposed to be riding. You're not worth keeping. You're all fired. Effective immediately."

"It wasn't me, sir," Carter blurted, his voice sounding desperate.

"Not me either," said Fred Walters, his face almost as white as his white blond hair.

Mr Ridgeway looked at Sid. Sid felt a trickle of sweat run down his back. He stared back at Mr Ridgeway. Surely the man knew he wasn't friends with this lot? There was no way he could explain.

Then Tyler spoke up. "It was me, sir."

Sid felt his knees go weak with relief. Mr Ridgeway stared at Tyler.

Tyler repeated, "It was me. Not that lot. They had nothing to do with it."

Mr Ridgeway raised his eyebrows.

"It's true, sir," said Tyler. "You can't blame any of them. It was me."

Mr Ridgeway eyed him. "You surprise me."

"Surprised myself, actually." He shrugged. "But you can't blame Everett. Can't blame my mates, either."

Mr Ridgeway looked at Tyler. "All right, Tyler. Thank you for your confession. They're not fired, but you are. As of this instant. Get out of here. Pack your things."

Tyler hesitated.

"Now!" barked Mr Ridgeway.

Tyler flicked a glance at Sid. Sid tried to signal with his eyes that he was grateful. He hoped Tyler got the message. They all watched as Tyler turned and walked out of the stable, his head held high, and closed the door behind him.

Mr Ridgeway looked at the rest of the boys. "You stay. But you're all banned from the trials. Not one of you will compete."

Sid heard a sharp intake of breath from Carter.

"And consider yourselves lucky to still be employed here," said Mr Ridgeway. "Now get out."

Sid followed the other boys as they slunk out of the stable. He glanced back as he went. Mr Ridgeway was standing alone, looking at his horses.

"I don't blame him," thought Sid. "I would have done the same."

***

That night, once again, Sid couldn't sleep.

Banned from the trials.

That meant no chance of riding in the Cup race. Not this year, anyhow. Maybe never. How long could he keep on battling, with everything against him?

He felt cold, with one of his blankets missing. It was in the stable, hidden in Manawa's stall. And he couldn't get comfortable without his pillow, either. He knew it was his bitter disappointment that was keeping him awake, but he decided to retrieve his pillow and blanket. He climbed down from his bunk and headed over to the stable.

The wind's dropping, he thought dully. Not that it makes any difference to me. Not now.

He pushed the stable door open. It creaked as it swung wide. Inside, Sid could see the glow of a lantern.

He paused, then stepped inside and closed the door. All around him the horses breathed gently, their faces lit by a lantern on a high shelf. And below the lantern, Mr Ridgeway stood, his arm resting against the wooden post next to Manawa's stall. The muscles of his jaw tightened when he saw Sid. "What are you doing here?" he growled.

"I came to get my pillow and blanket, sir," said Sid.

"You what?" asked Mr Ridgeway.

"My blanket and pillow. They're in Manawa's stall."

Mr Ridgeway looked at him, waiting for more.

"I slept here last night, sir."

Mr Ridgeway stared. "You were sleeping in here? Last night?"

"Yes." Sid felt a flush of embarrassment rush up his neck and into his cheeks, and was glad of the darkness. "I couldn't sleep in the bunk room last night. And I thought, since I was going to be riding Manawa, I should, you know, spend more time with him."

Mr Ridgeway continued to stare.

But I need my pillow and blanket back now," Sid finished lamely. He realised as he spoke that his story sounded strange.

"And the other boys?"

"They didn't sleep in here," said Sid.

"Not likely that they would," snorted Mr Ridgeway.

"I went to get my breakfast," said Sid. "And an apple for Manawa. And when I got back here, they came in," said Sid.

"You're an extraordinary boy," said Mr Ridgeway. He studied Sid. "Maybe you are the right one to ride Manawa." He pondered for a moment. "I'm rethinking my ban on you boys being in the trials."

Sid's heart leaped.

"I can't afford to lose you, or Carter," said Mr Ridgeway. "Or even Walters. Walters should have his chance." He stroked the side of Manawa's neck as he spoke. "I called Tyler's parents in, and he told them the whole story in front of me. Seems like he was the only one playing with matches. Trying to play the big man, and frighten everybody."

Mr Ridgeway snorted. "Well, he frightened me, that's for sure. He won't be back here. Ever. And I doubt if any other stable will have him now." He hesitated. "But he showed a bit of maturity, admitting what he'd done. I told him that. Hope it sank in."

"Has he gone home, sir?" asked Sid.

"Yes. His parents took him away. They were angry about taking him home. But we can't allow that sort of thing."

"No, sir," said Sid.

"It disappointed me, Sidney, seeing you hanging around with that lot. I expected better of you. Gerald Thorndon thought highly of you."

Sid said nothing.

"But now I know what really happened. You weren't with them. You were here alone, and they surprised you."

Sid kept his mouth shut.

"Well, you won't rat on the others. But I see how it was." Mr Ridgeway smiled. "All right, young Everett. I'd been looking forward to working with you. I thought it was going to fall through, but now it looks like it's still going to happen."

Sid smiled back at Mr Ridgeway. "That's good," he said.

"Off you go, then," said Mr Ridgeway. "Back to your bunk room. I'll give the word to Mr MacDonald that you're back in the trials."

"Thank you, sir."

Sid hesitated.

"Is there something else?"

"Can I just get my blanket and pillow, sir?"

"Oh, yes," said Mr Ridgeway. "Of course you can."

Sid climbed over into Manawa's stall and grabbed his rolled-up blanket and his pillow.

"You're a real horseman, Everett," said Mr Ridgeway. "I believe Daker is going to enjoy working with you." He nodded. "Good night."

"Good night, Mr Ridgeway," said Sid.

Sid couldn't stop smiling all the way back to his bunk room.

It was only when he'd climbed up onto his bunk bed and snuggled down again, that he noticed the silence. The wind had dropped. The nor'wester, which had hammered them for four days, was over. His heart lifted. He would be back to training in the morning.

Chapter
Twenty-Three

Wade Daker

Sid blinked in the sunlight. He'd almost forgotten what it felt like to stand straight, instead of hunching over against the wind. A fly buzzed lazily past his face, and found a place to rest on the sunny front steps of the Ridgeway's main building. Sid looked at the grass beneath his feet. It lay flat and withered – burned dry, as it would have been at the end of a long, hot summer.

"Everett?"

Sid looked around.

Mr Ridgeway was approaching, and with him was a short, athletic-looking man with a white plaster cast all the way down one leg, and a wooden crutch under one arm.

That has to be Wade Daker, thought Sid. He hurried over to meet them.

"Good morning, Everett," said Mr Ridgeway.

"Good morning, Mr Ridgeway."

"Wade, this is Sidney Everett. Sidney, Wade Daker."

Sid looked at Mr Daker. He had a suntanned face and thick brown hair. His eyes had creases at the corners as though he often smiled.

Mr Daker held out his hand. "Pleased to meet you, Sidney."

"Pleased to meet you," said Sid, shaking the man's hand.

"So you're the boy who's going to take on the big black? My old mate Manawa?" Mr Daker continued.

"I hope so, Mr Daker," said Sid.

"Call me Wade. I'm not old. Yet." Mr Daker gave Sid a lop-sided smile.

"I'll try," said Sid, knowing he wouldn't. He knew that at forty-five, Wade Daker was one of the oldest jockeys racing in New Zealand. He was also one of the best.

"Let's see him." Mr Ridgeway led the way, slowing his pace for Mr Daker. Sid could see that the plaster cast was heavy, and that Mr Daker couldn't bend his knee. He had to use his crutch, and swing his leg from the hip to move along.

"What a thing to happen, eh?" Daker said to Sid. "It's messed up my racing season. And no more rock climbing for me, for a while. But hey, maybe it was meant to be. What do you reckon? Someone up there telling me it's time to retire?"

"Never," said Mr Ridgeway.

"I'm sure it'll get better, Mr Daker," said Sid.

"Not such an easy mend, at my age," said Mr Daker. "Kids can break bones and their bones mend in no time. It's not so simple as you get older."

Sid glanced sideways at the leg, encased in thick white plaster.

Were things sometimes 'meant to be'? Was that true?

Mr Ridgeway led the way to the track, where Mr Te Waka waited with Manawa.

Sid caught his breath. Manawa gleamed in the sunlight; his head held high. His back was long, and his broad chest was built for strength and stamina. He whinnied as they approached.

"Mōrena," said Mr Te Waka. "He's pleased to see you, Wade. He's been missing you."

"Missed me, have you?" Wade Daker reached up a hand to stroke the glossy black neck. "I've missed you too, mate," he said. He ran his hand along the length of Manawa's back and glanced at Sid. "Look at that long back. He's a big boy," he said.

Sid nodded. He felt small, next to the gigantic horse. His heart was beating hard, and there were butterflies in his stomach as big as bats.

"I'll give you a leg up," said Mr Ridgeway.

Mr Te Waka handed Sid the reins, and he found himself sitting high on one of the top racehorses in the country. He stroked Manawa's neck, and looked down into the expectant faces of three men.

"See?" said Mr Te Waka. "What did I tell you?" He looked at the other men. "None of the other boys could get on him just like that. This boy has something special."

Mr Daker peered up at Sid. "He likes you, Sidney. No doubt about it. He'd have had you off by now, if he didn't think much of you."

"You'd be lying on the ground," agreed Mr Ridgeway.

Mr Te Waka gave Sid a wink. "You've got the knack, eh, boy?"

"He's been taking time to get to know the horse," said Mr Ridgeway. "That's the sign of a rider who cares." He looked at Sid. "All right. Let's see you ride."

Sid gulped. This was it. He nudged his heels into the horse's flanks, and they moved off, walking across the grass. Pressing Manawa into a trot, they moved further out.

Mr Ridgeway yelled, "All right, Everett. When you're ready."

Sid pressed his heels into Manawa's sides again, moving him into a canter. He glanced back at the watching men, then urged Manawa into a gallop. Together, they thundered around the track. It was as if Manawa had been holding himself in reserve, waiting to unleash his full power and strength.

Sid's heart sang as the exhilaration of speed pumped through his veins. He could hear Manawa's hooves drumming on the dry ground beneath them, and the warm breeze brought the fragrance of the fields wafting to his nostrils. The ground flashed beneath them, the withered grass a blur of brown and gold.

Sid crouched low, hovering above the saddle, the muscles in his legs straining as he rose and fell with the horse's movement. He had to hold himself back from letting out a whoop of joy as he and Manawa thundered over the ground. Far above, he could hear skylarks warbling in the blue sky. The sunlight dazzled his eyes, and glinted on Manawa's glossy mane.

This feels perfect, he thought. I feel like I'm flying.

As he rounded the circuit, he slowed, and brought Manawa back to a trot as they approached the men. He felt a grin spreading all over his face, and he reached down to pat Manawa's neck. "Well done, boy."

Manawa snorted.

Sid laughed. "Not enough, eh?"

He walked Manawa right up to the trio of men and reined him in to a stop, then looked down at them, waiting. He wasn't sure what to expect. It was hard to know what they were looking for. He had ridden like he always rode, feeling like he and the horse were one. But somehow, it felt even better, riding Manawa.

"Ka pai," murmured Mr Te Waka.

"Not bad, Sidney," said Mr Ridgeway.

Mr Daker gave him a quizzical smile. "You've got what it takes. Good form. And Manawa's got good form. Now, what we need is to get you both into top form."

Mr Ridgeway cleared his throat. "Everett, Mr Daker has offered to work with you and Manawa. Get you both ready for the Cup. With Mr Te Waka's assistance, of course."

Sid's heart leaped.

"If we pull this off," said Mr Ridgeway, "you'll be the youngest rider in New Zealand ever to enter. And hopefully, to win."

"Trained by the oldest," said Mr Daker. He grinned at Sid. "Reckon you're ready for it?"

"Yes, sir!" said Sid.

Chapter Twenty-Four

The Perfect Team

Wade Daker tipped back his cap, studying Sid. "You're doing well," he said. "The early morning gallops are paying off beautifully. Manawa just eats up two miles. And you're a natural. Not only that, you're always eager to learn. You're willing to try and try again. That's what sets you apart."

"And he's got a gift," said Mr Te Waka. "He's the right rider for Manawa."

"You should know. You trained him from a colt," said Mr Daker.

"Yes. And I trained you, Wade." Mr Te Waka's eyes crinkled up at the corners as he smiled.

"Yup," said Mr Daker. "You made us a team."

"And now, the magic's happening again," said Mr Te Waka, his eyes on Sid.

Sid squirmed. They were far too full of praise, those two. He himself was full of apprehension. But he knew that once he was seated on Manawa, all his anxiety would disappear. He would know what to do.

All his training, and his instincts, came into play, and the intoxication of riding a powerful horse, combined with the excitement of a big race, was irresistible. He and Manawa almost flew.

"Off you go then, Sid," said Mr Daker. "Once more, then we'll call it a day. Remember – you're one with the horse."

Sid walked Manawa out to the line and waited. He rubbed a hand across his face, feeling the sweat and dust sticking to his skin. He could do with a drink of water. Manawa seemed as fresh as he had at the beginning of the morning. Sid smiled.

Amazing staying power this horse has, he thought.

Mr Daker raised an arm, looking down at his stopwatch. Sid felt his heartbeat quicken.

Daker's arm dropped, and Sid and Manawa leaped forward, thundering once more around the track.

Sid felt the wind rushing past him as they flew across the ground. The pounding of hooves on the hard earth beneath him drummed in his ears, and around him, the dazzle of green trees and wooden fences flew by in a blur of colour.

Manawa always seemed to understand what was required, and he gave all his strength to a race. And hardly seemed tired afterwards. They circled the track, passing Mr Daker and Mr Te Waka at top speed, then slowed. Sid turned Manawa around and walked him back.

The two men watched them approach. They were silent, their faces serious. Sid's heart, already thudding in his chest, began to pound a little harder.

What was wrong?

Then the men looked at each other and grinned wider than Sid had ever seen them grin before. Mr T took off his felt hat, Wade Daker removed his cap, and they waved them in the air, whooping and laughing.

Mr Te Waka wiped a tear from his eye. "This is the real thing," he said. "I'm proud of you, son. And proud of you too, Manawa. A prince among horses."

"The trials will be just a formality. And the Cup is going to be quite a race," said Mr Daker.

Chapter Twenty-Five

The Trials

The agents and owners started arriving even before the horses were led out. It was a day of clear skies and bright sunshine, with a gentle breeze blowing. The nor'wester was already a distant memory. Only the dust lying in every nook and cranny reminded everyone of that ferocious and unrelenting wind.

Sid waited on the sidelines, holding Manawa's reins, waiting for his race. Sam was in the first race, mounted on Lady Kate. Sid's heart lurched as he watched Sam make his way onto the track. The riders wore no colours, but each wore a white cotton bib with a number, front and back. The bibs were tied on with cotton tapes that fluttered in the wind. Sam was number 10. He was far away along the line. Sid could see his bright ginger hair standing out like a beacon amongst the other jockeys. He could almost see the pink sunburn on Sam's freckled nose getting redder.

The agents stood huddled together, their hats pulled low over their eyes. Mr Ridgeway stood near them, his bulky figure looming conspicuously in a dark blue suit. With him was Wade Daker, and another smartly suited man who seemed to have his eyes not on the line-up, but on Sid.

Sid felt slightly unnerved.

Who was that man? And why was he staring? He tried to ignore the man's gaze as he gathered his courage and his concentration. Finally, a chance to show his worth. Although, actually, he was still unsure of his worth.

He reached out to Manawa, standing beside him, and stroked his silky neck. He looked up at the horse, a smile hovering at the corners of his mouth. Manawa's coat gleamed in the sunlight, his eyes were bright, his ears pricked in anticipation. He stamped a hoof, his skin twitching at the annoyance of a fly landing. Sid flapped a hand to shoo it away, and squinted out into the blazing day.

He remembered Wade Daker's words. You're one with the horse. Why wasn't that helping?

He clutched Manawa's reins, murmuring to him quietly the words of encouragement he badly needed to hear himself. Manawa was the best – he gave everything he had. Sid had absolute confidence in his horse. He just wasn't so sure of himself.

He had tried to ignore MacDonald's and Carter's put-downs. But as he waited for his race to start, he felt less confident with every passing moment. The sun beat down on his shoulders, making him feel weary before he even climbed up into the saddle. Standing there, surrounded by horses and riders, he felt isolated by his fears. A block of ice had settled in his brain, blurring everything that was usually clear.

He became aware of someone beside him. Matt. He stood there, seeming to be completely relaxed. He had that aura of calm, like Mr Te Waka.

"I can see Sam out there," said Matt.

"Can't miss him," said Sid.

"You up next?" Matt asked.

"Yup," said Sid. A shiver of anxiety ran down his spine as he spoke. He wished he felt as confident as he sounded.

"Manawa won't let you down," said Matt. He reached out and rubbed Manawa's neck.

"Yeah, I know," said Sid.

Matt glanced at him. "You'll be fine," he said. "I've seen you ride. You've got what it takes." He stood in his steady way, watching the horses, his dark hair blowing straight back from his face.

Sid studied him surreptitiously. He had noticed Kiri talking with this young man.

Not that Kiri means anything to me. She's just a girl who works in the kitchen.

"Thanks," he muttered.

"If you need water after the race," said Matt, "the cooks have put a canteen on the table over there. No reason why we should all get parched, waiting around in the heat."

Matt nodded his head towards a trestle table. The water canteen was a large metal container with a tap that hung over the edge of the table. "I'm getting a tray of glasses from the kitchen," he said. "Save the cooks from coming back out here." He sauntered off towards the kitchen.

Sid stared after him, trying to squash down his feelings.

Jealous?

Kiri was nothing to him. He hardly knew her. Sarah was his girl. And Sarah was coming down here soon. He needed to keep his thoughts away from Kiri and Matt.

None of my business, he said to himself.

Manawa whinnied and stamped his foot again.

"I know," said Sid, reaching up to stroke his silky neck. "It's not fun waiting, is it? But we'll be racing soon."

Kiri approached, wearing her kitchen apron. "If you need water after the race," she said, "we've put a canteen on the table over there."

"Yeah, I know," said Sid.

Kiri raised an eyebrow.

"Um, thanks," said Sid. "We'll need water."

She swung away, walking with an easy stride towards the kitchen. Sid felt a twinge of something else.

Longing? No. He took a few slow breaths. Focus on the race.

He turned his attention back to the line-up. Sam was looking his way, and he gave him the thumbs-up signal.

The countdown began, and the crowd fell silent, waiting for the off.

The starter pistol cracked, and the horses leaped forward, their riders hunching low. Sid noticed that Sam was off to a good start, his number 10 visible in the front bunch of horses, his red hair flaming.

Sid's heart pounded as he watched them thunder along the straight, the bunch spreading out. The ground shuddered as they approached, making his heart beat even faster. The horses roared by, their legs stretching out, flashing past in a dazzle of speed and power. Then they swept away along the track, reaching the curve at the far end and bunching up again.

They were too far off to read any of the numbers now, but Sam's flaming red hair always showed where he was. He was near the front and moving up.

The horses spread out along the far side of the track, then rounded the curve. They were returning now, heading for the finish line. Sid moved forward, closer to the barrier. The bunch of agents also shifted, craning their necks for a better view.

As the horses crossed the finish line, Sid noticed out of the corner of his eye that Kiri had returned, and with her was Mr Te Waka.

Kiri punched the air. "Yes!" she shouted. "Go, Sam!"

The agents were making notes in their notebooks. Mr Ridgeway pulled out a white handkerchief and wiped the sweat from his face and neck. He looked pleased. That was good. The man next to him was staring at Manawa.

Who is he? Sid wondered again.

The riders were leaving the track. Sam approached, leading Lady Kate.

"How did you go?" asked Sid. "I couldn't see what happened at the end."

"Third," said Sam. "I did pretty well. And so did Lady Kate. Didn't you, girl?" He patted his sweating mount. "The agents noticed Lady Kate. They're watching form. They like to see the winning line-up, of course. First, second and third. But they take in everything." Sam's face was shining with sweat.

"There's water over there," Sid pointed.

"Good! I'll grab some," said Sam, "and then I'll watch your race."

Sid swung himself up into the saddle, gathered the reins, and walked Manawa towards the track.

As he passed Mr Te Waka, Mr T called out to him. "Kia kaha, Sidney!"

Sid grinned. "Thanks, Mr T. We'll do our best."

His heart lifting, he took his place in the line-up. Some horses were stamping and swishing their tails, some standing quietly, their ears pricked. Manawa was a quiet one. He stood still, but fully alert. Sid felt his tension and sensed his awareness that a race was about to begin. He would put his heart into it, he knew.

A breeze wafted across the track, cooling Sid's face. He glanced up at the clear blue sky. A breeze was much appreciated.

He squinted his eyes, listening for the starter, trying to calm his pounding heart. This was important. He had to do well.

Chapter Twenty-Six

Sid's Race

Sid cast a glance left and right along the line. There was Fred Walters, his white-blond hair clearly visible. And not far away, Carter. Carter turned his head, meeting Sid's gaze with a mocking curl of his lips, then looked away.

Sid turned his head, staring at the track ahead, waiting for the start. The race was about to begin.

The starter raised his hand for silence. He was counting down. Sid could see his lips moving, but he couldn't hear a word. Then the pistol cracked.

Manawa shot away, like the true racehorse he was. Sid barely had to press his heels against his flanks. He felt a wild burst of excitement as they leapt into the lead. Right from the start, they were at the head of the bunch.

Sid bent low, crouching in the California Crouch that jockeys the world over now used. It gave an extra edge, relieving the horse of the rider's weight momentarily, as he lifted into the air again and again.

As they thundered along the track, Sid felt the exhilaration of speed coursing through his veins. The air was sweet as it rushed into his lungs. Manawa's hooves thudded on the turf, and he could hear the distant shouts of the onlookers. The track was a blur.

"Come on, boy! Come on! We can do it!"

With his mouth parched, Sid's voice wasn't much more than a croak. He could hardly hear himself, and felt anxiety clutch at his heart. But Manawa had heard him. He powered ahead, his legs flying out, his muscles straining. They swept around the curve at the far end of the track, almost floating. Sid's sense of exhilaration returned as they moved into the straight on the far side.

Sid was gasping, his heart hammering, the blood pounding in his ears so loudly that he couldn't hear anything else. He was aware of the other riders bunched around him and behind him, threatening to overtake. But Manawa still held the lead as they flew into the final straight.

"Well done, Manawa," he gasped.

Sid realised he was grinning as he rode. He'd never led all the way through a race before. It felt incredible! He didn't dare to glance behind or beside. His peripheral vision told him that Carter was creeping up beside him. Catching up inch by inch until he was almost flanking him. He was just a neck behind, but Sid was pretty sure that Carter's move was too late.

He yelled again; the wind pouring into his lungs as he opened his mouth, threatening to stifle his words. "Come on, Manawa!"

Manawa responded, straining every muscle as they swept across the finish line, an entire length ahead of Carter's horse, and far ahead of the other riders.

As they slowed, voices came to his ears. Shouts of congratulation. He turned his horse, leaning down to stroke Manawa's sweaty, dusty neck. "Well done, Manawa," he murmured.

He walked Manawa back to where Mr Ridgeway and Mr Daker waited, sensing everyone's eyes on him. Sam was waving and grinning, his face glowing like a tomato. And next to Sam, Kiri was waving, too. He felt his heart flip, then noticed next to Kiri, the tall figure of Matt.

Him again.

Quickly, he turned his gaze back to Mr Ridgeway.

"Gerald Thorndon wasn't wrong," said Mr Ridgeway, as he reached Sid's side. "Your old boss is an excellent judge. He said you knew how to get the best out of a horse."

"That was nice of him," Sid stammered.

"I'm surprised he let you go," said Mr Ridgeway. "You could have done a lot for his stables. I wonder why?"

Sid kept his mouth shut. He knew the answer to the unspoken question, but he wasn't going to say.

"Oh well," said Mr Ridgeway. "His loss is my gain. You're riding Manawa in the New Zealand Cup." He turned to the man next to him. "Charles? Allow me to introduce Sidney Everett." He looked at Sid. "Sidney, meet Mr Charles Bellingham, Galahad's owner."

It was the man who'd been staring at him. Sid had heard of Galahad, another horse tipped to win the cup. "Hello," he said.

"Nice riding," said Mr Bellingham. "I wasn't sure what to think when they told me a sixteen-year-old boy was taking over from Wade Daker." He nodded at Wade. "You picked a good one," he said.

"I think Manawa picked him," said Mr Daker, grinning.

Sid desperately needed a drink of water. He began to move away.

Sam, Kiri and Matt approached. "What did Ridgeway say?" asked Sam.

"I'm in!" Sid felt a flush of heat flood his face. "He said I did well. And I'm riding Manawa in the New Zealand Cup!"

"I knew it! You deserve it," said Sam. "Couldn't have been a better trial."

Sid grinned. "It wasn't too bad," he agreed. He tried not to look at Kiri, but she planted herself in front of him.

"Well done!" she said. "Not bad for someone who's not from the Mainland." The teasing sparkle in her eyes challenged him.

Sid wished he could think of a clever reply, but nothing came to him.

Sam elbowed him. "Come on, mate, let's get our horses sorted out."

"I need a drink of water," said Sid. "And I'm sure Manawa needs one too."

They walked away side by side, leading their horses.

***

At the wind-down party, Sid accepted a glass of lemonade, and helped himself to chocolate cake. Mrs O'Brien winked at him. "I hear you did yourself proud today," she said.

Sid beamed at her. "I've never led a race all the way around before."

Mrs O'Brien studied him, her head on one side. "So, you'll be riding him in the Cup? That's what they're saying."

"Yup," said Sid.

"Somebody's nose will be out of joint," she murmured.

Sid glanced around before replying. "Yeah, I think Mr MacDonald will be mad. And Carter. But Mr Ridgeway is happy – that's what matters." He hesitated. "And I've got my big chance."

"You deserve it, Sidney," she said. "It hasn't been easy for you."

"True," admitted Sid. Nothing had been easy since he'd moved to Ridgeways.

Mrs O'Brien added, "And not many people can handle that big black brute."

"Brute?" said Sid. "That's no way to talk about Manawa. He's a champion. Born to win."

"In the right hands," Mrs O'Brien said wisely. "I may be only kitchen staff, but I know what it takes. My brother was a jockey, back in the day."

"Was he?" said Sid.

"Yes. He told me it's not just all about the horse. It's about the rider, too. He said it takes skill and determination, plus a certain amount of luck. But what really matters is the rapport between the horse and rider. People don't always know that. The punters pick the horses, but it's the jockeys who get the best out of them. I've never forgotten that."

"Yeah," said Sid. "He was right." He hesitated. "I hope I can do as well on Cup Day as I did in the trial."

"You can do it, Sidney," said Mrs O'Brien.

Sid pulled a face. "A lot could happen on the day. A lot could happen even before the day.

"You'll be the youngest ever to ride in the New Zealand Cup," said Mrs O'Brien. "That's what they're saying. Did you know that?"

"Yes," said Sid.

"Good luck," she said. "We'll all be listening to the wireless, willing you to win. Now I'd better put out some more sandwiches. They're going fast."

As she headed back to the kitchen, Sid felt an elbow dig into his side. He turned to see Sam, his mouth full, waving a sausage roll with a big bite out of it.

"Look over there," Sam mumbled through his mouthful.

Sid's eyes opened wide. Kiri, in a red dress, sashayed through the crowd, ignoring the admiring looks from the jockeys and agents. She made a beeline for Sid.

"Nice going, cowboy," she murmured, and then burst out laughing. "Sorry," she gasped. "I was trying to do something I saw at the pictures. But I can't keep a straight face."

Sid smiled. "It was looking pretty good," he said, "until you laughed."

Kiri looked abashed. "I just wanted to say, 'well done'. It's not every day you see someone lead a race from start to finish."

"It's not every day you get to ride a horse like Manawa," said Sid. "He's amazing."

"Yeah, he's pretty special. And so is his rider." Suddenly flushing, Kiri spun on her heel and hurried away, heading for the kitchen.

Sid stared after her.

"Put your eyes back in your head, Sid," said Sam.

"I wasn't staring."

"Right," said Sam.

"She's not usually that friendly," said Sid.

"Or that dressed up," said Sam.

A minute later, Kiri was behind the counter, a scarf over her dark curls and a white apron covering her dress.

"Back to normal," said Sam.

"Looks like it," agreed Sid. But nothing seemed normal.

I'm in the Cup, he thought, dizzy with excitement, a huge wave of gratitude flooding his heart.

And Kiri...

He abandoned that second line of thought. Who knew what Kiri was up to? One minute she was furious with him, the next minute she was being really friendly. He sighed.

The Cup. Sarah is coming down to watch the Cup race.

That was what mattered. He had to focus on the race, only a week away. It was his big chance, and he didn't need any distractions.

Chapter Twenty-Seven

Vigilantes

On the night before the Cup race, Sid couldn't sleep. Anticipation of the event filled his thoughts. The big day. Finally. His family was coming to watch. And he'd be riding Manawa. He stared wide-eyed into the darkness, adrenaline coursing through his veins.

Sam's snores didn't help, either. He had to get some fresh air. Climbing down from his bunk, he took care not to step on Sam, sleeping below, his arm flung out as usual. He tiptoed across the floor, opened the door, and stepped outside into the cool darkness of the night.

The grass was wet with dew under his bare feet. Crickets trilled nearby, and in the distance, moreporks hooted. The vast, inky expanse of the sky was awash with a billion stars, the long sweep of the Milky Way spiralling across it.

It reminded Sid of his long-ago night rides with Mr Thorndon's horse, Silver, following the dusty moonlit lane to the wild, west coast beach in the dead of night.

He shook off the memories. They weren't all good.

A murmur of voices came to his ears. Who else was awake at this hour? He glanced around the darkened grounds. Lights were glowing in one of the bunk rooms – the room Carter and his mates occupied. Instinctively, Sid moved towards the sound, creeping up to the building. The windows were open, but the curtains were closed. The voices floated out clearly on the night air.

"Yeah, a hobo or something. Living rough." It was Carter's voice.

"In the industrial area?" someone asked.

"Yeah. In a derelict building. My uncle told me. He's organising a search party to look for him," said Carter.

"Why?" asked another voice.

"Can't have hobos and vagrants, can we?" said Carter. "Stands to reason. Lighting fires. Endangering the city. Endangering the stables. It's not far away. It's a threat."

"How is it a threat? It's not near the stables." That was Walter's voice. "It's on the other side of the forest."

"So?" said somebody else. "That forest could burn. It could burn all the way to here."

"So, he's going there with the dogs," continued Carter. "Uncle Angus and his mate."

"Sounds like a laugh," said another voice.

"It's not a laugh," said Carter. "It's serious. Uncle Angus is going to run him out. Send him packing. We don't want his sort around here."

"When is this happening?" asked somebody else.

"Tomorrow morning," said Carter. "It's a free day, tomorrow, because of the Cup. Just the horses to look after. My uncle told me."

"Are you going, Carter?" someone asked.

"Me? Not likely. The Cup race is tomorrow," said Carter.

Sid could hear the pride in Carter's voice. It made his blood boil. What right did they have to run a man out of his hiding place? The man wasn't doing any harm.

Kiri. Sid's heart beat faster. This man must be something to do with Kiri. He'd have to warn her.

She can't keep me out of it now. In the darkness, he clenched his fists. We can ride there together. We'll get there first. Those idiots will get there and find nobody.

Carter was cackling with laughter. "Yeah. Uncle Angus's dogs are pretty good at sniffing out vermin."

The other boys in the bunk room all started talking at once. Sid couldn't make out what they were saying, but he got the gist of it. There was trouble brewing, and luckily, he had a chance to head it off. And to warn Kiri.

Sam. I'll need Sam.

He headed back to his bunk room to wake his snoring buddy.

***

"Why did you have to wake me up?" Sam sat up in bed, scowling. "I was having a fantastic dream."

"No time for dreaming, Sam. This is serious." Sid could hear panic in his own voice, and steadied himself. "We need to help somebody."

"Who?" asked Sam.

Sid outlined the danger, and saw Sam's face change from grumpy to worried.

"Those dogs are mean," said Sam. "They're hunting dogs. Mac-Donald and his mate take them pig hunting down south."

"All the more reason to start early, and to be careful how we go. We'll tell Kiri first thing in the morning. Don't let her put us off. She'll need help."

"Sid! You can't do anything about it," said Sam.

"Why not?" asked Sid.

"Because you're riding Manawa in the Cup. That's why."

"I haven't forgotten," said Sid. "How could I forget that? I can't sleep for thinking about it. But this is important."

"Get some sleep," said Sam.

"Where does Kiri stay?" asked Sid. "She doesn't stay here. She stays somewhere else."

"She stays with Mrs O'Brien," said Sam. "They get here at four, to start the breakfast." He looked at Sid. "Go back to sleep, Sid, and we'll wake up early. We'll warn her. Then you can get ready for the Cup race."

Sid climbed back up to his bunk and lay down. "I wish I had a watch. I haven't had any sleep yet, and I might not wake up."

"To wake up at four o'clock, bang your head on the pillow four times," said Sam. "That always works."

"What? Really?" said Sid.

"Yes," said Sam. "That's what my mum always says."

"Never heard that," said Sid. "But it's worth a try."

He banged his head on the pillow four times. "Actually, I think it might work," he whispered. "I feel sleepy already." He closed his eyes.

Chapter Twenty-Eight

To The Rescue

S id woke to pitch-black darkness. His senses told him it would soon be dawn.

"Sam," he whispered. "Wake up!"

Sam groaned.

Sid tugged on his clothes. "Hurry, Sam," he said in a loud whisper.

The boys raced to the cookhouse. Sid felt goosebumps break out on his skin. There had been a change in the weather since last evening. The dazzling sky full of stars had disappeared. The wind was coming from the west, and low banks of cloud had rolled in, completely obscuring the stars. As they reached the door of the canteen, the first drops of rain fell.

Sid banged on the outside door to the kitchen.

Mrs O'Brien opened the door. "It's a bit early, boys," she said. "Can you come back later?"

"We're not here for food, Mrs O'Brien," said Sid. "It's about the man hiding in the industrial estate."

Mrs O'Brien's kindly face filled with alarm. "How do you know...?"

"We overheard a conversation," said Sid. "The man's in danger. People have found out about him. Mr MacDonald, and some others. They're going up there with dogs to flush him out. To get rid of him."

Mrs O'Brien's face paled. "Come inside, boys," she said.

Mrs O'Brien fixed the boys with a stern look. "Tell me what you know."

"I know Kiri has been taking food to someone," said Sid. He glanced at Mrs O'Brien for confirmation. She nodded, not saying anything.

"I've never mentioned it to anyone," said Sid. "Until just now, when I told Sam. But somehow, Mr MacDonald found out about him. We want to warn him. Kiri needs to warn him."

"Kiri isn't here," said Mrs MacDonald. "She suspected they were planning something. One of them made some kind of nasty remark that sounded like a threat, and she's already gone to warn Daniel. She's moving him to a different hiding place. I suppose you know who Daniel is?"

"She called him 'Uncle Dan'," said Sid.

"He's her uncle, from Dunedin," said Mrs O'Brien. "The one who was in the papers."

"The one who left his wife?" asked Sid.

"It's not like it sounds," said Mrs O'Brien. "He left because he couldn't cope with normal life after the war. He was a prisoner of war..." Mrs O'Brien shut her mouth, pressing her lips tight together.

"It's all right, Mrs O'Brien," said Sid gently. "You don't need to tell me. We just wanted to warn Kiri, so she could tell him."

"She already knows, Sidney," said Mrs O'Brien. "Leave it to her. You've got the Cup race to think about." She hesitated. "But if there are dogs…" She bit her lip. "To be honest, I'm worried. If there are dogs, they'll find him."

"We should tell Mr Ridgeway," said Sam. "Or the Police."

"What would Mr Ridgeway do?" said Sid. "And the Police would take too long. We'll help her, then hurry back. We've got time."

Mrs O'Brien frowned. "I suppose. But the Cup…"

"Leave it to us, Mrs O'Brien," said Sid. "Have you got anything that dogs might like? To distract them? Something to put the dogs off the scent."

"Oh, yes, we've got leftover stew."

Mrs O'Brien opened the door into the pantry and came out with a large tin, with 'Greggs Ground Pepper' written on it. "This is almost empty," she said. She took a pot from the fridge and ladled cold stew into the tin until it was full. She pushed the lid back on tightly.

Sid grabbed the tin. "Thanks, Mrs O'Brien," he said. "If anyone asks, you don't know where we are."

She gave him a look of concern.

"Don't worry," he said. But he could feel Mrs O'Brien's anxious gaze on his back as they left.

***

Sid and Sam hurried back to their bunk room, pulled on oilskin jackets, and stashed the tin of stew in a leather satchel. Then they ran to the stable. Sid found Lady Kate and led her outside, while Sam found her saddle and bridle. In minutes, they were ready. Sid swung himself up into the saddle and put his arm down to help Sam up. Sam sat behind with the leather satchel on his back.

Sid didn't hesitate. He galloped Lady Kate along the track towards the kahikatea forest, following the same path Kiri usually took, Sam clinging on tight behind him. The darkness was fading. How soon would MacDonald and his dogs set off?

Sid slowed the horse to a walk as they entered the gloom of the forest, following the path between the trees. He closed his eyes tight, then opened them again, trying to adjust his vision to the leafy darkness. A bird, startled by their presence, clattered up from the branches of a tree. Sid glimpsed it as it swooped overhead. Raindrops were trickling through the treetops and pattering on the ground. The fragrance of damp earth and mossy branches filled his nostrils.

He urged Lady Kate from a walk into a trot.

As long as the path is wide, he figured, and the branches of the trees are high up, it should be fine. Hopefully.

"Are you sure it's safe to go this fast?" Sam called from behind.

"I hope so. We can't waste time," Sid yelled back. "In fact, I think we should go faster." He pressed his heels into Lady Kate's flanks, urging her into a canter.

Flying through the woods with Sam clinging on behind him, Sid had an eerie flashback to another desperate ride. That time, he had been the one clinging on behind in a terrifying ride by moonlight, a frantic charge through the darkness to rescue an injured horse.

Sid reined in his imagination. Get a grip on yourself. This isn't the same. This time, you're with a friend, not an angry neighbour. And this time, it isn't your fault.

They powered through the woods, the horse sure-footed, even at speed.

"She's as good as a mule," gasped Sam.

Sid didn't know a lot about mules. He'd heard they were stubborn and bad-tempered. "Yeah," he agreed. "She almost seems to know her way."

The path widened, and the trees thinned out. Sid slowed Lady Kate to a walk. They were at the end of the forest, and gloomy outlines of vast, hulking buildings rose before them.

Which building was Daniel in?

They crossed a small, stony wasteland, then a parking area in front of a modern railway workshop. Two big old buildings stood nearby, their boards rough and bent, with some of the window glass broken.

"These buildings look empty," said Sid. "He could be in one of them."

He dismounted, tying Lady Kate to a rickety wooden rail, under the shelter of a wooden awning. He gazed around. Raindrops drummed on tin roofs. A door creaked as it swung in the wind. Then he saw a light glowing, spilling out through cracks in the wooden walls.

"There!" he whispered.

He crept over to the building, with Sam following close behind. He pulled the door open, and they stepped inside.

They tried to walk quietly, but their footsteps echoed in the vast darkness of the building. It smelt damp and musty. The floorboards sagged and creaked underfoot as they moved forward. Here and there, sizeable holes gaped in the floor.

"Be careful," whispered Sid. "We could easily go through."

They made their way through a huge, gloomy space, then along a dark passageway and through a series of dusty, empty rooms. A rustle in the corner of one room made them freeze.

"Rats?" suggested Sam.

Sid peered into the gloom, wishing he had some sort of light. Some old boxes leaned against the wall, with a few rags poking out. "Yup," he said. "I reckon."

At the far end of the building, Sid opened the exterior door. He turned to Sam. "No sign of anyone," he whispered. "Maybe we got it wrong. Maybe the light was in the next building."

Stepping outside, they found a dead campfire. Raindrops plinked into a dirty enamel plate. An old, silver tablespoon lay on the ground next to a billy tipped over onto its side. A notebook was spread open to the sky, the pages absorbing the raindrops, now falling fast.

"He cooked here," said Sid. He looked up at the building opposite. It was an old stable, with a gaping hole in the wall. "Perhaps he slept in there?"

Sam stooped and picked up the notebook, scanning the open pages. "It looks like poetry," he said. "The ink's running. I'll rescue it."

Sid knelt to examine the muddy earth. Boot prints covered the ground; boot prints large and small. "There are two sets of prints here," he said. "It's Kiri and her uncle. It must be."

The sound of approaching hoofbeats made them spin around.

"Quick," said Sid. "Hide!"

They pulled open the door into the old stable building and rushed inside, Sam still holding the notebook.

The hoofbeats slowed to a walk. Sid peered out through a crack in the wall.

A horse and rider rounded the corner of the building. Sid gasped. It wasn't Mr MacDonald, or any of that gang. It was Matt. Matt, the one who made Sid's blood boil whenever he saw him with Kiri.

Matt slid down from his horse and headed straight towards them. He seemed to know where he was going.

Sid turned to Sam and saw his own bewilderment reflected in his friend's eyes. "Matt," he whispered. "Now what?"

Before Sam had time to answer, Matt burst into the room. He glared at Sid and Sam. "Where is he?" he demanded.

"Who?" asked Sid.

Matt said, "My dad."

Chapter Twenty-Nine

The Hobo

S id stared at Matt. "Your *dad*?"

"The hobo is your father?" asked Sam.

Matt snorted. "He's no hobo."

"He's Kiri's uncle," said Sid.

"Yes," said Matt. "And he's also my dad. He came to Ridgeways to find me. But then he couldn't face meeting people, so he found this place to hide out." Matt looked away, his face twisting. "He didn't even want to see me. But he lets Kiri come here and bring him food. I think she reminds him of his sister."

Sid felt a few things click into place, like pieces of a jigsaw puzzle.

Matt looked back at Sid and Sam, rubbing the side of his face. "Kiri's my cousin. It's been like a game, for her. An adventure. She just brought him a letter from Mum, now that Mum knows where he is. It's all been a big secret. Until you started nosing around."

"I wasn't nosing," said Sid.

Matt glared. "I don't know what else you'd call it." He lifted his chin, not taking his eyes off Sid. "I don't know if your dad went to the war? Well, mine did, and he was captured. He was a prisoner of war in Java, and he's been through hell."

Matt's dark eyes were no longer focused on Sid. He seemed to be looking at something far away.

"Is that why he's hiding?" asked Sam.

Matt nodded. "My mum says he brought the hell back with him," he said. "He had nightmares. He didn't want to see anybody. Then he vanished. It was in the newspapers. He turned up here, and said he didn't want to go back. This has been his safe place ever since."

"My dad was in the war," said Sid. "But just the normal war."

If there is such a thing as a normal war, he thought.

"He wasn't captured," he added.

"Anyway," said Matt. "The point is – where is he now?" He stared wildly around. "Dad!" he yelled. "Dad, where are you?"

A faint voice answered from somewhere in the building; a girl's voice. It was Kiri.

"He's here, Matt! He's here. But I can't wake him."

The three boys stared at each other, then ran. Sid's heart thudded in his chest as he followed Sam and Matt, hurrying through the huge, echoing building towards the sound of Kiri's voice.

In the middle of another vast, empty room, Kiri knelt next to a man lying on the ground, his eyes closed, his shirt unbuttoned.

She raised a stricken face towards them as they approached. "He's not answering me. He's not waking up."

Matt dropped to his knees beside her. "Dad!" he said, his voice urgent. "Dad, it's me. Matt." He picked up the man's hand, lying limply on the ground, and rubbed it. "Dad, can you hear me?"

The man stirred, his eyelids fluttering. Kiri's eyes met Sid's. Then she bent her head again, her long dark hair swinging like a curtain across her face. Sid couldn't hear what she said. But when she raised herself back up again, her eyes were full of tears.

"It's okay, Dad," said Matt. "You'll be all right."

The man's eyes opened and blinked. "Matt?"

"Yes, it's me, Dad." Matt's voice shook.

"Uncle Dan?" Kiri touched the man's arm. "Matt will help you get some warm clothes on. You have to get away. People know you're here. People who don't like it that you're here." She buttoned up his shirt. "Uncle Dan? This is serious. You need to come to Ridgeways. Mr Te Waka is happy to…"

"No!" the man shouted. His thin body shook as a fit of coughing seized him. "No. I'm going up to the cave."

Sid looked at Matt. "Cave?"

"Dunno," said Matt. "Maybe he's remembering something? Somewhere he hid when he escaped from the prisoner of war camp?" He crouched down next to his father and touched his arm.

"All right, Dad. That's fine. Just get some warm clothes on. That's all you need to do right now." Matt's voice was soothing. He was talking to his father as if he was the dad, and his father was the boy.

A wave of pity welled up in Sid's heart, followed by a swell of gratitude. At least his own dad had come back from the war okay. Well, fairly okay. A lot more okay than this.

Just then, a distant barking reached his ears. The dogs! In his concern for Daniel, he'd forgotten the imminent danger.

He turned to Sam. "They're coming," he said. "We have to get him away right now!"

"I'll take him," said Kiri. She lowered her voice to a whisper. "I've got Mr Te Waka's horse. I'll lead Uncle Dan through the building and out the other end. Then we'll ride for Ridgeways. You boys stay here and delay them."

Sam reached a hand inside his shirt, and pulled out the notebook he'd retrieved from the puddle. He held it out to Kiri. "Your uncle's book, I think."

Kiri took it, flashing Sam a grateful smile. "Thanks, Sam," she said. She stowed the book in her bag, and pulled out an oilskin jacket. She helped her uncle to his feet, assisted by Matt. "Here, Uncle Dan. Put this on."

She and Matt helped him into it, as if he was a child. Then she took her uncle's hand. "Are you able to walk, Uncle Dan? We're going to the cave. I'll bring your breakfast with us. All right?"

Daniel gave her a bewildered look. "The cave?"

"Yeah, your hideout cave," said Kiri. She searched his face with anxious eyes.

"Oh, yes. My cave." A faint smile lit up Daniel's weathered features. "Yes, they won't find me there."

"We're going to ride there on a horse. Alright?"

Daniel lifted his chin in assent. "Alright," he said.

She held his arm, guiding him. Daniel's footsteps were slow and painful.

Sid watched them go; his heart heavy. Then he heard shouts outside and spun around. The hunters were here. The vigilantes. He could imagine the dogs straining at their leads, and the mean faces of Mac-Donald, his hunting buddy, and the others. "Let's barricade the door," he said.

The voices and the barking of dogs grew louder.

"What with?" asked Sam. "And it's too late, anyway."

"The stew!" said Sid.

Sam swung the satchel down from his back, undid the straps, and lifted out the tin.

Sid prised off the lid, and poured the fragrant stew in long trails across the floor. "That'll hold them up," he grinned.

He dropped the tin, and he, Sam and Matt braced themselves to meet the approaching mob.

Chapter Thirty

Distraction

Mr MacDonald was the first to burst into the building, with a snarling dog straining at the end of a lead. A second man followed with the other dog. Some of Carter's mates were behind them, but there was no sign of Carter. The men advanced into the echoing room, their boots marching across the trails of stew, glaring at Sid and his friends. Behind them, the rest of the group of boys pushed their way inside.

"So, what brings you here?" asked Matt.

"What brings us here?" asked Mr MacDonald. "Getting rid of vermin, that's what." He glared at Matt. "What brings you here, Connolley?"

Matt stood with his shoulders back, his face calm. He was as tall as Mr MacDonald, Sid noticed, and his shoulders were broader.

"There's no vermin here, Mr MacDonald," Matt said. "My father has been living here. And now he's gone. You've missed him." He raised his chin. "And he's not vermin. He's my father."

The dogs, who had been eagerly licking up the stew on the ground, began to whine and shake their heads.

Sid stared and then concealed a smile.

There was a lot of pepper in that stew, he thought.

Mr MacDonald stared at the dogs. They were rubbing their noses with their front paws, yelping and whining.

"What have you done to my dogs? You've poisoned my dogs!" he shouted.

"I don't think pepper is poisonous. Not last time I looked," said Sid, stepping up next to Matt.

Mr MacDonald advanced towards Sid and Matt, his face flushing red with rage. "He's got to go. He's a menace to the community. His camp is a fire risk."

"You should listen to yourself," said Matt. "Afraid of a lone man hiding out in an old building. Afraid of a man who isn't doing you, or anyone else, any harm."

"Matt's dad is a returned soldier," said Sid. "Like my dad. Like lots of dads. Some of them need a bit more time to adjust to life back home, that's all."

Matt flashed him a grateful glance.

"Yes," said Matt. "A bit of time. That's all he needs. Attacking him isn't going to help."

"Out of our way, Connolley," said Mr MacDonald. "I've got no fight with you. I'm just going to tell your old man he has to move on. That's all."

"You won't be doing that," said Matt quietly.

"You going to stop me?" snarled Mr MacDonald.

"Yes," said Matt. "I am."

MacDonald handed his dog's lead to a boy in the group and raised his fists. The two men circled each other, the young man and the old, fists ready, watching for an opening. The others closed in, like a pack of wolves. Sid and Sam stepped back to confer.

"Sid," said Sam. "Get going. Follow Kiri and her uncle. I'll stay here and help to hold this lot off."

"Won't they see me go?" asked Sid. "And follow me? I'll lead them straight to him."

"They're watching a fight," said Sam. "I don't think they'll notice. If they do, I'll delay them. You can help them get to the cave."

Sid stared at his friend. "I don't think there is a cave, Sam. I think that's all in his mind. But I'll find them."

Mr MacDonald and Matt continued to circle around, fists raised and eyes narrowed.

Nobody noticed as Sid slipped away into the darkness, closing the door to the passageway behind him.

The yells of the boys grew fainter immediately.

Good for Sam, he thought. He hoped Matt would win, and wished he could be there to see it. He would have liked to see MacDonald get his comeuppance.

Chapter Thirty-One

The Well

Outside in the blustery semi-darkness, Sid stared around him, catching his breath, trying to see where he was. It was a sort of alleyway between the derelict buildings. Wind whistled around the rooftops. Moonlight shone through ragged clouds, reflecting off puddles on the uneven ground.

"Kiri!" He tried to make his whisper as loud as he could. "Where are you?"

A snort and a stamp made him spin around. A horse – tied up and alone. He could see spots on its flanks. Appaloosa. It was Mr Te Waka's horse. So where were Daniel and Kiri?

"Kiri!" he whispered again. The moon disappeared behind the clouds, and he was plunged into darkness.

"Sid, is that you?" Kiri answered. Her voice carried faintly to his ears, as if it was coming from another world. Her voice sounded sort of tight and strange too, as if she was in pain. She *was* in pain, Sid was sure of it.

Kiri's voice came again. "Be careful. I've fallen down a hole in the ground. I think it's an old well."

"Are you hurt?" Sid strained his eyes in the darkness. "I can't see any hole in the ground."

"Watch out or you'll fall in too," she warned.

"Where's Daniel?" Sid asked.

"He ran off," said Kiri. "He seemed to get his strength back, all of a sudden. I couldn't get him on the horse. He figured out where I was taking him. I tried to find him, and next thing I knew, I'd fallen down this well."

"Keep talking," said Sid. "Let me hear where you are."

"I don't know what to say."

"Sing, then. Or something. Make a noise."

There was a moment's silence, then Kiri started singing. "Twinkle, twinkle, little star..."

Sid could have laughed, but he didn't. He strained his ears, trying to find the direction her voice was coming from. He dropped to all fours and crawled.

The singing stopped.

"Keep singing!" he said.

"I feel stupid." Kiri's voice was closer – it seemed to come from somewhere almost directly below him.

"You'll feel even more stupid if you die down there," he told her.

"I can't feel stupid if I'm dead."

"You'd be the stupidest ghost that ever haunted anywhere," said Sid. "Keep on singing."

"I'm not going to die. You're going to get me out."

Kiri started singing again, this time a haunting, magical melody. Me He Manu Rere – like a bird that flies.

The words seemed to float up to him from another, older time, and it sent shivers down his spine.

He tried to keep his voice steady and reassuring. "That's good, Kiri. That's really good. I'm close. I've almost found you. Keep singing. I'll get you out, and then we'll find your uncle. OH!"

Sid's right hand had reached out and touched nothing but empty space. He was on the brink of a gaping hole in the ground. He'd almost fallen into the well himself! There it was, right in front of him. He peered into the inky blackness, but could see nothing. The opening was all but invisible until he was right on top of it.

The singing had stopped.

"Kiri?" he said. "I think I found you. I almost fell in."

Her voice echoed up, loud and clear. "Good you didn't!"

"Yup," said Sid. He stared around. Daylight was growing, revealing the outlines of the old buildings. The rough, muddy ground was still in darkness. He got to his feet carefully. There was nothing to grab hold of. Some broken concrete pillars gleamed nearby, but they were a bit too far away to be useful.

He knelt down again, next to the hole. "Can you see any light?" he asked. "Can you see anything at all?"

"What do you mean?" asked Kiri. "I can see a faint, grey light at the top of the hole, where I fell in. I can't see your stupid head, which is just as well. Keep back, or you'll fall on top of me."

Sid noticed that the other side of the well had a broken edge, and the bricks lining the inside of the well were uneven. "I think I can see a way to climb down," he said.

"Don't you dare!" shouted Kiri. "You mustn't try to come down here! Get help!"

"I'm coming down." Sid lay on his stomach and peered down the hole. "How deep is it?"

"How should I know?" said Kiri. "I can see your head now. Don't come down."

"How long were you in the air?" he asked.

"In the air?" said Kiri.

"I mean, when you were falling," said Sid.

"Oh," said Kiri. "I timed it with my stopwatch."

"What?" said Sid.

"I'm joking, you dummy. How would I know how long? It seemed like forever, but it wasn't long, really." Her voice shook. "I think I've cut myself. I touched my arm, and it's all sticky. It's blood. And it hurts. You need to get help."

Sid scrambled to his feet, looking around, and then jumped. A pair of steady grey eyes were staring straight at him. Someone was standing right there, his hair and beard glowing red in the faint light of early dawn. Daniel was holding a rope. Sid hadn't even heard him approach.

"Hello, son," said Daniel. "Is that my niece down there?"

"Yes," said Sid.

He doesn't look crazy. He looks calm. And that rope is exactly what I need.

"I'll help you get her out," said Daniel. "I'll belay you." He raised his eyebrows. "Have you ever been belayed, boy?"

"Belayed?" said Sid.

"Lowered down on a rope."

"Oh," said Sid. "No. But I can do that."

"Good," said Daniel.

Uncle Dan went to the edge of the dark hole in the ground and leaned over. "Are you all right, young Kiri?" he called.

"I'm okay!" Kiri's voice echoed up from the darkness.

"Good," said Daniel. "We'll soon have you out of there."

Uncle Dan tied the rope around Sid's middle, looping it around several times. "What's your name, son?" he asked.

"Sid," said Sid. "Sid Everett."

"Well, Sid," said Daniel, "this is a bowline knot. You'll have to undo it when you get to the bottom. And you'll have to tie it around Kiri. So let me see you untie it and then tie it again."

Sid stared at him. "Won't we both come back up together?" he asked.

"I can't pull the two of you up at the same time," said Daniel. "I don't have the strength. It'll have to be one at a time. Kiri first." He looked at Sid. "I'm not as strong as I was," he said gruffly.

Sid felt anxiety twisting around in his stomach. This man had been barely conscious, a short time ago.

"You'll have to trust me," said Daniel. "I won't leave you down there. I promise."

"No," said Sid. "Of course you won't."

He felt Daniel's eyes watching his hands as he untied the rope and tied it again.

"That's good," Daniel said. He made Sid repeat the exercise with his eyes shut, just to be sure. "You need to know how to do it, even without being able to see what you're doing," he said. "This will give you a picture, in your mind. We don't want any problems down there in the dark, do we?"

He watched as Sid retied the rope around his waist one more time, then ran a length of it across to one of the broken concrete pillars. He looped it around that, then wound the rest of the rope around his own body.

"Right. We're ready." Daniel looked at Sid. "Lie on your stomach next to the hole. Hold on to the rope with both hands. Then swing your legs over. Try to find a toehold. If you can't find one, I'll let you down, anyway."

Sid lay on his stomach next to the well, grasped the rope in his hands, then swung his legs over. He stared up at Daniel Connolley. The man seemed absolutely calm and reassuringly normal.

"All right," said Sid. "I'm ready."

"Good," said Daniel. "Feel for the wall with your feet."

Sid kicked around with his legs, reaching for something solid. His toes found the edge of a brick jutting out from the circular wall. He pressed on it with his foot, to test it, and it held firm. "I found something."

"That's good," said Daniel. "I'll lower you down. Bounce yourself off the sides of the well. The bricks won't go down very far. Then there'll be stones, or rock. Try not to let yourself spin around. I'll lower you slowly, and you yell out when you're ready to move down, or if you want me to stop."

Chapter Thirty-Two

Spinning In Darkness

S id tried not to spin in the darkness at the end of the rope, reaching with his feet for a solid surface. His boots scraped against something, and his heart lurched with relief as he planted them against the curved brick wall of the well.

"Okay," he yelled up.

As the rope let out, he bounced off; the cord cutting into his hands as he gripped tight. His breathing echoed back at him in the enclosed space, and the circle of dim light above him grew a little smaller.

His feet found a solid wall again.

"All right. Let me down a bit more!" he yelled to Daniel.

Each time the rope let out, Sid swung and bounced off invisible surfaces. He abseiled down in short, terrifying bursts, dropping into the depths of the well.

"How are you going down there?" Daniel's distant voice reached his ears like a person calling to him from another world.

"I've got the hang of it," Sid called back. Then, peering into the blackness below him, he called, "Kiri? Are you okay?"

Kiri's voice echoed up to him, sounding closer now. "I'm fine. I can see you against the light. You look like a giant wētā, all creepy, with your legs sticking out."

Sid grinned in the darkness. She had her sense of humour back – that was good. And her voice sounded less strained. The rope let out again, and he lurched downwards, his stomach taking a second to catch up, as his feet bounced against the wall.

"You're nearly at the bottom!" Kiri's voice was close now.

"Nearly at the bottom, Dan!" he yelled up to his belayer.

It was very dark down here. What if Daniel left them at the bottom of the well?

Kiri spoke, her voice coming from just below him. "You can trust Uncle Dan, Sid. He'll get us back out."

The next drop, his feet touched solid ground. He staggered and stood upright. "I've reached the bottom, Daniel," he called. He took a step, and something crunched under his boot.

"They're bones," said Kiri. "Very small bones. I accidentally put my hand on them. Rat bones, I think."

Sid strained his eyes to see, but the darkness was absolute. A drip, drip, drip of water nearby reached his ears.

"It's a dry well," said Kiri. "Fortunately for me."

She had to be standing right next to him, but Sid couldn't see anything. He looked up, and saw the mouth of the well far above, a tiny circle of dim light, shining in the overwhelming darkness.

A hand touched his shoulder.

He jumped.

"Welcome to wētā world, Sid," said Kiri.

"Wētā world?" said Sid, his skin crawling at the thought.

"You know you can get those cave wētās?" Kiri asked. "With the really long legs, and the extra-long feelers? I'd recommend that you don't touch the walls down here."

Daniel's head appeared in the circle of light far above them – a slight bump on the dark edge of the well.

"Everything all right, down there?" he asked.

"Hi, Uncle Dan," called Kiri. "Sid's at the bottom. What do we do now?"

"Sidney?" called Daniel.

"Yes?"

"You'll have to untie yourself now, and tie the rope around Kiri, like I showed you."

"I remember." Sid ran his fingers along his ropes in the darkness. He couldn't see a thing. The rope felt uncomfortably tight around his body. He fumbled for the end. Or for the knot. Somewhere to begin.

His fingers were clumsy. He could almost hear time passing, like the ticking of an alarm clock reverberating in his head. Panic rose in his chest, and he fought it down.

"Got it?" called Daniel.

"I... no!" Sid struggled in the darkness, trying to prise the ropes apart with his fingers. As the minutes passed, he felt sweat breaking out on his forehead, even in the chill subterranean air.

"Have you got a knife?" whispered Kiri. "You could cut it."

A knife. Yes! He had a knife.

Sid dug in his pocket and pulled out the knife Mr Thorndon had given him on that day he'd told him he had to leave. A flood of gratitude to his old boss welled up inside him. He prised open the blade, found the knot, and began to saw at the rope.

"What's happening down there?" Daniel's voice echoed down from above.

"Sid's cutting the rope. The knot's too tight," answered Kiri.

There was silence from above.

"There isn't much rope to spare. We've used the entire length of it," Daniel said, eventually.

"It's okay, Daniel," Sid called back. "I'm only removing the knot."

The last fibres of the rope parted, and the knot dropped to the cave floor. Sid found the newly cut end, and unwound the rope from his body. Then he reached out for Kiri.

"Your turn," he said.

He wound the rope around and around her waist, and tied the knot, as Daniel had shown him. He found he had a picture of the knot-tying sequence in his mind, just as Daniel had promised. His heart lifted.

"There you go," he said to Kiri. "Let him know when you're ready. He'll pull you up. Hold the rope with both hands and get your feet against the wall as soon as you can."

"Thanks, Sid," said Kiri.

"I'm ready!" she yelled up to Daniel.

"See you at the top, Sid," she said, and began her ascent.

Chapter
Thirty-Three

Daniel Connolley

S id watched Kiri's silhouette grow smaller and smaller as Daniel belayed her up. Her feet bounced off the rock wall as she ascended, and her long hair swung out with each spring of her legs.

Just like a wētā, he thought, grinning to himself in the darkness.

He noticed that one of her arms sometimes hung loose – she was occasionally holding onto the rope with only one hand.

She's injured! He'd forgotten. She said she was bleeding. Feeling like an idiot, he watched as she reached the top and was hauled to safety. Then the rope snaked back down through the darkness to land at his feet.

Winding it around his waist and knotting it securely, Sid yelled to Daniel that he was ready. As the rope tensioned, he began the ascent, moving upwards through dense blackness, then through shadowed grey until he reached the top. Relief washed over him as he put his hands on the edge of the well, grasping for something to hold on to.

Daniel's hands grabbed his arms, and Sid felt himself being hauled over the edge to safety. For a few moments, he lay with his eyes closed, listening to the wind whistling around the old buildings. He opened his eyes to see daylight.

"Just as well I didn't plan on a career in mining," he joked. He sat up and looked around for Kiri.

Kiri sat cradling her arm. In the morning light, he could see that one sleeve of her blouse was soaked with blood, and her skirt was stained with dark blotches.

Daniel crouched down next to Sid. "She's lost a bit of blood," he murmured. "I don't know how much. But she needs a doctor."

Sid stood up, allowing Daniel to untie the rope from around his waist.

Daniel coiled the rope carefully. Then he eyed Kiri and Sid. "All right, you kids. Time for you to go."

"And time for you to come with us, Uncle Dan," said Kiri.

Daniel stared at her. "Nope," he said. He set his mouth in a thin, determined line.

"Yes," said Kiri, getting to her feet. "It's time. Time to stop this. Those people tried to hunt you down. They were going to run you out of here, and they won't stop trying. They'll do it again. It's time for you to come home."

"I'm not ready," said Daniel. "I'm just not ready. Your auntie understands."

"Yes, she understands. She'll wait for you. But you can't stay here." Kiri hesitated. "Come to Ridgeways. Mr Te Waka has a bed for you and everything." Her tear-filled eyes were pleading.

Daniel was about to answer when footsteps crunched on gravel. He spun around, taking a fighting stance.

With a wave of relief, Sid recognised Sam and Matt.

***

Matt walked over to his father. "Hello, Dad," he said.

Daniel stared at him, wooden-faced. Then a smile softened his features. "Good to see you, son," he said. He reached out a hand and touched Matt's shoulder.

Matt's face lit up with relief. "You too, Dad," he said.

Sam was leading Lady Kate. He dropped the reins, leaving them trailing. "What happened here?" he asked. "Kiri's covered in blood."

"She fell down a well," said Sid. "We got her out. Watch where you walk – it's right here."

Sam spotted the circular hole in the ground. "Crikey," he said. He hurried over to Lady Kate, snatched up her reins and tethered her to a railing. Sid joined him, as Matt went to kneel next to Kiri.

Sam grimaced at Sid. "Scary!" he said.

Sid tipped his head towards the derelict building. "What happened back there?" he asked.

"Matt's not bad in a fight," said Sam, a small smile twitching up the corner of his mouth. "He might have a few bruises. But he gave MacDonald something to think about. It was mostly dodging blows, but he managed to get him good in the stomach a couple of times."

Sid smiled. "Are they gone?" he asked.

"They've gone back to Ridgeways," said Sam. "The fight was a brilliant distraction – nobody saw you go until it was too late." He grinned. "I don't think Daniel will have any more trouble from Mac-Donald."

Sid looked at Matt, who was with his father and Kiri. They looked like they were arguing.

Sam chuckled. "Everyone's going to hear about it. There aren't many secrets at Ridgeways."

"Kiri's trying to persuade her uncle to come back with her to Ridgeways," said Sid.

Sid and Sam turned to see that Daniel had folded his arms, his face grim. Matt stared at him for a long moment, then turned away. He helped Kiri up onto the back of Mr Te Waka's horse, and swung himself up into the saddle in front of her. Kiri put her arms around him. Sid could see that the arm in the blood-stained sleeve wasn't able to hold on very well.

"Looks like they're giving up," Sid muttered. "Wait!" he called. He hurried over. "Mr Connolley?"

Daniel Connolley eyed him coldly. "What?"

"My dad was in the war, and when he came home, he found it hard to adjust to civilian life. I know it's tough."

Daniel raised his eyebrows. "Where did he serve?"

"Crete. He served in Crete," said Sid.

"Captured?" asked Daniel.

"No," said Sid.

"I was in the Pacific," said Daniel. "I ran into the Japanese. My war ended pretty quickly."

Matt slipped back down out of the saddle, handing the reins to Kiri, and came over to stand beside his father.

"I did nothing except stay alive," growled Daniel.

"You stayed alive. That's the important thing. We're so glad. And you escaped. That's brave," said Matt. "That took courage."

Daniel shuddered. In the moonlight, Sid could see that his face was pale and sweating.

"And you looked after your mate. You got him to safety, too," said Matt.

"He died in the jungle." Daniel rasped out the words. "I had to leave him there."

"Nobody blames you, Dad," Matt said. "He died a free man. And it was thanks to you. You're just as much a hero as any other man who fought in the war. You all fought for freedom." Emotion choked Matt's voice. "You fought, and you won, no matter what part of the world you were in, and no matter how your war turned out. And I'm proud of you." His voice cracked, and tears spilled down his cheeks.

"Come back with us," he pleaded. "Mr Te Waka has a room ready and waiting for you." He looked at Kiri, who nodded, then back at his dad. "It's peaceful there. Nobody will bother you. Mr T trains horses, and I do a lot of that too, these days. We could use some help."

His dad seemed to be listening, so Matt kept on talking. "There's an injured horse that needs someone to walk him around. Show him a bit of kindness. And a kid who needs someone to show him that not all dads are mean." He hesitated. "And when you're ready, Mum will come and see you. And take you home. If you're ready for that."

Daniel stared off into the distance. Sid held his breath.

After a long moment, Daniel spoke again. "Maybe you're right, son," he said, looking at Matt. "If the old fella's got room for me..."

"He has!" said Matt, his face breaking into a huge smile. "He's got room for you, and he told me he'd appreciate your company."

Matt turned to Sid. "Sid, can you ride with Kiri? Take her back? I'm going to walk back with my dad."

Chapter Thirty-Four

Too Late

S id rode Mr Te Waka's horse right up to the door of the cook-house, followed by Sam on Lady Kate, and sprang to the ground. He helped Kiri dismount, noticing that she winced in pain. She held her arm stiffly, trying to protect it.

Everything was strangely quiet. Where was everyone?

"I'll find Mr T," said Sam. "Tell him who's coming to visit him." He rode off on Lady Kate towards the trainer's quarters.

Sid banged on the cookhouse door.

Mrs O'Brien opened the door, took one look at Kiri and scooped her into her arms. She hurried her inside. "I'll phone the doctor, Sidney," she called over her shoulder. "I'll tell them I'm bringing her in." She eyed Sid sadly. "You're a good boy, Sidney, but I think you've blown your chance of riding in the Cup. You'd better get yourself to the racetrack somehow. Although I suspect it's too late. You can borrow my bicycle. Or maybe Mr T can take you. Pretty much everybody else has gone, except for you."

The racetrack. Riccarton. The Cup race.

Sid felt sick as he realised the awful truth. He'd been so focused on the rescue he'd completely forgotten about the Cup race. And now it was too late to get there. MacDonald would have the last laugh, after all. He could have wept.

Stiff upper lip, he told himself. There must be a way. But the flood of sickening disappointment gave way to despair, filling up every corner of his heart. They would have replaced him by now, for sure.

He leaned against the cookhouse wall. Skylarks sang high above him in the clear morning air. It was usually his favourite sound in all the world.

Mrs O'Brien burst out of the building again, with Kiri. "Come on, Sidney. I'll take you there in the truck. Apparently, Mr T is expecting a visitor. Kiri's insisting that I get you to the races first, and then she'll see a doctor after that. I can't stand around arguing with her. Come on, we'll use the truck."

Sid's heart leapt. He led Mr Te Waka's horse to a shady spot and tied him up. "Thanks," he whispered to the horse. "Wish me luck!"

Mrs O'Brien led the way to where the stable's Bedford truck was parked. She reached a hand under the curve of the mudguard. "The key is usually on top of the tyre," she said, and fished it out.

Sid stared. "Can you drive?" he blurted out.

"Don't look so surprised," said Mrs O'Brien. "I was a driver in the WAAF during the war. I'm a very good driver." She helped Kiri climb up onto the front seat, her arm wrapped in a tea towel. "Hop in, Sidney," she said.

Sid climbed in next to Kiri, inhaling the smell of sun-warmed vinyl. It reminded him of his dad's car. He wondered if his family was there at the races, all waiting to see him ride.

But they might not see me ride, he thought.

Mrs O'Brien pulled out the choke, turned the key in the ignition and pressed the starter. The truck roared into life, and she put it into gear. "Hold on tight," she said, and accelerated down the long Ridgeways driveway, heading for Riccarton Racetrack.

Chapter Thirty-Five

Riccarton Racetrack

Mr Ridgeway frowned as he peered down at the racetrack through his binoculars. The line-up was taking far too long to establish. Where was Manawa? And where was Sidney Everett, his rider? This couldn't go wrong. He had all his hopes pinned on this race. Not to mention a considerable amount of money. It just couldn't go wrong...

Glancing sideways, he took in the satisfied expression of his friend Charles Bellingham, racehorse owner and investor in Ridgeways.

Blast the man, he thought. *He never puts in any work. Just pays the money.* He sighed. Oh, well. It was money that made the world go round. The racing world, in particular.

"Galahad's looking good, Charles," he said cheerfully, hiding his anxiety.

"Oh, yes," murmured Bellingham laconically. "Gally's a grand lad. He always puts on a good show. I just hope he'll put on a good burst of speed at the required moment. Leave your Manawa in the dust." He chuckled complacently. "He rarely lets me down."

Charles Bellingham raised his binoculars to his eyes. "Where is Manawa? I thought you told me I was going to eat my hat today. Eat it or lose it." He chuckled again. "Maybe it's you who'll be eating your words?"

***

Sid's family settled themselves in the grandstand. Dad had splashed out, as a concession to Auntie Glad, and bought everyone seats. Aunt Gladys wouldn't have managed in the crush at the rail where they usually stood, down on the grass beside the track.

"All right, Glad?" he asked.

"Right as rain," she answered, producing a tiny pair of binoculars from her handbag.

"Those are nice, Glad," said Mum.

Auntie Gladys grinned. "I've kept these for years, even after I married my Cedric. I've had them fifty years! I had a feeling that one day I'd be back at the races." Her grin widened. "I told Cedric they were for bird watching. And I did actually use them for that. Once. We had a pair of white herons arrive, and they made a nest by the river mouth. Beautiful, they were. All the way from Australia, apparently."

Aunt Gladys was in good spirits, enjoying the outing. Sid's mother was glad of the chitchat to calm her nerves before the race.

Beryl was studying the line-up. "There's something wrong," she said. "Sid should be in this race, riding Manawa. And they're not there."

"Are you sure it's this race he's in?" asked Mum. "It's easy to get them mixed up."

"Yes," said Beryl. She looked back down at her racing sheet. "It's definitely this one."

"What?" Dad leaped to his feet. "How can he not be there?"

"He's riding Manawa, right?" said Beryl. "The big black one? Well, he's not there. I can't see the horse, and I can't see Sid."

"There's a big black one right there, in the line-up," said Dad.

"Yes, but that's not the one," said Beryl. "Wrong number. And wrong colours. I know Sid's colours. He's wearing royal blue and gold. And Manawa is number seven." She paused, studying the horses on the track below. "Nice horse, though, that other black one." She looked back at her racing sheet. "Number eight. He's called 'Galahad'." She clenched her fists. "Oh, where is Sid?"

Dad squinted up at the line-up board. "Manawa's name is still up there. He hasn't been scratched. So, what's going on?"

***

Beside the track, in the holding area, Mr Ridgeway's groom walked up and down with Manawa. He scanned the crowd anxiously.

Where was that wretched boy, Everett?

It's the age, he told himself. He might have the riding skills, but he hasn't got the maturity. Can't even show up for a race that would be the making of his career.

He called one of the stable boys.

"Find Mr Ridgeway. He'll be in the box, up high in the stand. You know what he looks like?"

"Yes, sir," said the boy.

"Tell him I'm replacing Everett with Carter. Unless he wants his horse scratched from the running. And I'm sure he won't want that."

"No, sir." The boy rushed away.

Chapter Thirty-Six

Horse Whisperer

Sid leaped down from the truck. "Thanks, Mrs O'Brien," he shouted, and slammed the door. He raced for the stable.

"I'm here!" he shouted. There was no answer. The stable seemed to be empty, but he could tell that at least one horse was still here. From inside, a clatter of hooves rattled and boomed in the echoing space, and a shrill neigh lanced out into the air. Manawa! It was him - it had to be. He didn't like strangers.

Sid rushed inside.

In the centre of the stable, Manawa lunged and reared, snorting and neighing. His flanks were heaving, his eyes rolling. His hooves pawed high in the air as he reared and whinnied in his distress. Two grooms desperately grasped ropes to keep him in check.

Mr Ridgeway stood nearby, his face crimson with rage.

Cowering against the wall, Carter shielded his face with one arm. "He won't let me near him," he yelled to Mr Ridgeway.

"It's useless," said Mr Ridgeway bitterly. "He's got himself into a state. We can't enter him. He'll have to be scratched from the line-up."

Sid walked forward quietly, his heart beating fast. "Manawa! Easy, boy."

Manawa pricked up his ears and turned his sweating head towards the sound of Sid's voice. Sid stepped forward. He kept talking, keeping his voice gentle, allowing the words to pour out into the dusty air, soothing and calming the agitated horse.

Manawa snorted and pawed the ground. Sid stepped a little closer. Manawa snorted again, shaking his head. Sid reached up a hand and touched the sweating neck. "Here I am, boy. I didn't let you down. See? I'm here." He continued to speak soothing words, then turned to Carter.

"I'll wear those silks."

Carter blinked, and then nodded. He unbuttoned the colourful jacket and threw it to Sid. Then the cap. The groom pulled the Number 7 bib over Sid's head and tied the ribbons. "Go," he said. Sid swung himself up into the saddle, patting the broad black shoulder of the horse beneath him as they rode out onto the track.

A cheer went up as the crowd saw him arrive.

Two stewards came to meet Sid and lead him to his starting place. Breathing hard, Sid and Manawa took their place in the line-up.

Mr Ridgeway wiped his forehead with a linen handkerchief and made his way back to the grandstand.

Chapter
Thirty-Seven

The New Zealand Cup Race

The starter pistol cracked and Manawa leaped forward, placing himself in the leading bunch right from the beginning.

Sid rose and fell with the rhythm of the horse's powerful movement. The focus of his mind narrowed down to one thing: the race. He sensed Manawa lengthening his stride. He and Manawa moved as one. They had an affinity. A bond. Sid didn't understand it – it was a kind of magic that happened with horses. He crouched low, eyes narrowed, his determination to win informing every move he made.

He glanced to his left. Galahad, the other black, was close to the rail, powering ahead of the grey that shadowed him. Galahad was owned by one of Mr Ridgeway's mates, Sid knew. He wouldn't be the only one worried about the outcome of this race.

Above his head, the commentator's voice crackled from the speakers. It was a blur of noise echoing around the stadium, unintelligible to a rider.

Sid leaned forward. "Go, Manawa!" he shouted. Intoxicated with speed, and with the power of the horse beneath him, Sid gave his whole heart to the race. The roar of the crowd filled his ears, the hooves of a dozen or more horses thundered on the track, and the smell of the turf filled his nostrils. The ground flickered dizzyingly beneath Manawa's flying hooves.

They swept around the curve of the track at the far end; the horses moving in a close bunch. The crowd of racegoers standing close to the rail whipped past in a blur of colour, their shouts and cheers filling his ears as he flew by. The thrill of the race swept over him, as it always did. The excitement, the fight against the odds, the sheer joy of speed. He could feel Manawa's energy as they flew along the track. This horse was built for speed. And for stamina. A two-mile race took endurance. Manawa was doing what he was best at. Sid could have laughed aloud.

As the horses pounded down the straight on the far side of the track, Sid sensed the bunch spreading out. He and Manawa were in the smaller group leading the race. There were five, no, six horses, straining for the win, leaving the slower horses behind. But Sid knew better than to count those slower ones out. They could save themselves for a burst at the end. He kept his focus on Manawa – striving to get the best from him.

They hurtled around the curve at the other end of the track; the punters roaring encouragement; the commentary blaring. Billboards swept by as he passed, the advertising blurring into flickering colours of gold and blue.

Gold and blue. *Those are my colours.*

Sid felt a swell of pride, edged with anxiety. He seemed to have lost ground. Ahead of him, three horses had settled into the lead.

Galahad, the other black in the race, a silver grey, and a golden palomino.

"Come on, Manawa," he whispered. He pressed his knees into his horse's sides, urging him onwards, fighting against the anxiety that threatened to flood him.

Had the stress before the race sapped Manawa's energy? He'd been rearing up. Sweating. He'd been distressed. Maybe he couldn't recover from that in time to give his best to the race?

Images flickered through Sid's mind. Daniel's notebook floating in a puddle. The brick-lined well. Kiri's blood-soaked sleeve. The look on Matt's face when his dad agreed to go with him.

Sid thought, If I lose this race because of last night...

But he wanted to win. His determination came from the very core of his being. "We're going to win, Manawa," he muttered. "Come on!"

As if he understood, Manawa redoubled his efforts, picking up the pace, inching ahead until he was beside the grey and the palomino. Their riders flicked him sideways glances, then turned their eyes back to the finish line.

So close!

Manawa had caught the scent of victory; Sid was sure of it. He seemed to have found some extra strength from somewhere, some reserve he pulled from within himself. They were passing the grey and the gold and gaining on Galahad. As they rounded the curve of the track and entered the final straight, heading for the finish line, Sid's heart was pounding in his chest. His mouth was dry and his breath came in gasps.

Now they were neck and neck with Galahad. Sid glanced sideways at Gally's rider and caught his eye. The other jockey smiled grimly, urging his horse on towards the finish line.

Sid knew that Manawa was giving his all. Was it enough?

As they neared the finish line, Sid could hear the crowd roaring. His blood drummed in his ears. The world narrowed down to a brightly coloured, turf-scented corridor of hope.

The two black horses approached the finish line side by side, neck and neck. Sid pressed Manawa onwards, desperate for that vital advantage. A nose was all it took.

There was a tremendous roar from the crowd as they crossed the finish line, their cries rising like a wave.

Sid was gasping, dizzy with speed, and so churned up with emotion he hardly dared to listen to the results. On the board, the names were going up.

Manawa in first place. Galahad second. Honey, third, and Whisperer in fourth place.

Sid whooped, raising a fist high. "Manawa, we did it!" He pulled off his cap and leaned down, touching his forehead against Manawa's sweating neck. "We did it!" He hugged the horse's neck with both arms.

The announcer's voice crackled out over the loudspeakers, confirming the results on the board as the crowd burst into a storm of clapping.

In a daze, Sid rode Manawa back to the finish line, tugging his cap back onto his head. The stewards directed him towards the birdcage – the platform where the jockeys received their trophies.

As he passed the line of newspaper men, cameras flashed, and he knew his picture would be in the paper. His and Manawa's. He grinned as he thought of his dad, knowing he would proudly pin the newspaper cutting to the wall. Just as he himself had done as a young boy – following the famous jockeys, dreaming of the future.

Suddenly, there was a commotion, and the crowd of newspapermen parted to make way for Wade Daker, dressed in his usual casual suit and cap. Press cameras flashed as he approached.

"Mr Daker! A photo with Sidney Everett, please!" shouted a reporter. "Let's have New Zealand's most celebrated jockey alongside the newcomer, on the day of victory. What a picture!"

Sid stood with Wade Daker for the photograph, trying not to blink at the camera flashes.

"Well done, son," said Mr Daker. "I knew you had it in you. Manawa knew it too."

Sid nodded. His heart was too full to speak.

Chapter Thirty-Eight

Sarah

As Sid left the birdcage, his mind in a whirl, a groom came to take Manawa from him. He dismounted and handed over the reins. Feeling dazed and exhausted, he stumbled away, unsure of where to go next. People he didn't even know were congratulating him left, right and centre.

Then, ahead of him, he saw Sarah. She looked as beautiful as he remembered her.

"Hello, Sid," said Sarah.

"Hello, Sarah," he replied. His mouth was dry. "How are you?" he croaked.

"I'm fine." She smiled her dazzling smile, and Sid felt his heart swell as if it would burst. Then he noticed her dad was with her. Mr Thorndon, his old boss.

Mr Thorndon put his arm around his daughter protectively.

What's his problem? Surely I can have a little time with his daughter? Sid thought. He'd waited months to see her.

"Well done, Sidney," said Mr Thorndon. He held out his hand, and Sid shook it. "You've done yourself proud. And your father must be proud of you." He raised his eyebrows, making it a question.

"Yes, he is," said Sid.

"And your mother, I'm sure. How is she?" Mr Thorndon continued.

"Mum's fine," said Sid. He hesitated. "She's happy to be back here, where she grew up. She's looking after one of my old aunties now."

"An old auntie?" Sarah smiled.

"Yeah," said Sid, turning to her. "My Auntie Glad. I never knew I had an auntie down here. She's mad keen on horse racing."

"It must be in the blood," said Mr Thorndon. "Did your family watch the race?"

"Yes, they're here somewhere. All of them." Sid glanced around. His family was nowhere to be seen.

"Good for them," said Mr Thorndon. "A fine family, Sidney."

Sid felt his heart warming at the kind words. Mr Thorndon was a decent man. Just overprotective of his daughter...

Mr Thorndon patted Sarah on the back, stepping away. "I'll find John Ridgeway. He'll have a big smile on his face, that's for sure."

"Okay, Dad," said Sarah.

Mr Thornton frowned. "Sarah, remember, I'd rather you didn't use that expression."

"What expression?" she asked.

"You know," said her father.

"Oh!" Sarah rolled her eyes and turned to Sid. "He doesn't like me saying 'okay'. He thinks it's too American." She turned back to her father. "Dad, I've told you a hundred times. Everybody says *okay*."

"Well, I don't like it, and nor does your mother. We'd prefer you to say 'all right', like a well-brought-up young lady."

Sarah sighed, but smiled at her father. "All right, Dad."

"That's my girl." Mr Thorndon nodded at Sid and walked away.

Sarah rolled her eyes again. "Dad's such an old stick-in-the-mud," she whispered.

Sid grinned, beginning to relax. This was the Sarah he knew. "He's a good man," he said. "He cares about you, that's all."

Suddenly, a tall young man appeared at Sarah's side. He was smartly dressed, with his hair carefully combed to one side. He stood confidently, gazing at Sid with a questioning expression on his face. Sid noticed he stood very close to Sarah. Instinctively, he knew that this was bad.

"Um, Sid?" Sarah's cheeks had flushed scarlet. "I'd like you to meet David. David Bellingham. His family owns 'Galahad'."

Oh, thought Sid. Galahad. Owned by one of Mr Ridgeway's mates. And worth a fortune.

"How do you do?" David smiled at Sid. He had the easy, confident smile of the well-educated and rich. He touched Sarah's arm. "Shouldn't we be joining Mother?" he murmured to her. He looked apologetically at Sid. "Mother's bought ice creams, and I'm afraid they'll melt ever so quickly in this heat."

Sid thought maybe Sarah had flinched at the young man's touch on her arm. Maybe. But probably not. It was most likely his imagination. She seemed perfectly happy standing there. Just embarrassed.

So she should be, he thought angrily.

His heart sank down into his boots. He'd been waiting for so long. This should have been the perfect moment. But nothing was turning out like he'd imagined it. He stared at Sarah, and at this David person, standing next to her. Everything he'd hoped for had just disappeared in a flash. She had another life. Another boyfriend. He knew he'd lost her.

A million thoughts flew around inside his head as the truth sank in. He'd known it, really, deep down. Her letters had been getting shorter and less frequent. He kept his expression steady, not betraying his dismay, but trying to communicate without words his hurt, and his disappointment. Maybe he could communicate everything he felt through his eyes?

Sarah faltered under his gaze, her smile fading, then she put on a bright voice. "Okay," she said to David. "Oops, I mean all right."

She turned to Sid. "Congratulations, Sid. Well done. I knew you could do it." She flashed her old, achingly familiar smile. "I'd better go," she said.

Sid watched as she walked away, her blonde curls bouncing, the tall young man striding along next to her. He saw them take hands, just before he lost sight of them in the crowd.

Chapter Thirty-Nine

Winning and Losing

A voice behind Sid made him jump.

"Sid! Here you are! We've been looking for you."

It was Beryl. Sid tried to pull himself together.

"What's the matter?" she asked.

"I'm okay," he muttered.

"And I'm a monkey's uncle," she said. "What's wrong?"

Sid looked at his older sister. "I just saw Sarah," he said. "And I don't think I'll be seeing her again."

"Oh, Sid!" Beryl's eyes filled with sympathy. "I knew something like this would happen. Well, I didn't know, but I wondered. With the way things were, it wasn't impossible. You being so far away, I mean. For so long." Her voice trailed off awkwardly.

"She obviously thought so." Sid kicked at the ground. "I might have known. I sort of suspected. She didn't write to me very often, anymore." He felt his throat tighten up, and suddenly he didn't trust his voice.

"Oh, Sid," said Beryl again. For a moment, they just looked at each other.

"Life, eh?" she said.

"Yeah," said Sid. "Oh well. I can't blame her. She can do better than picking someone like me. She's rich and everything."

"Nobody could do better than picking you, Sid," said Beryl. "You're gold. She just wasn't the right one, that's all."

Suddenly, the rest of the family surrounded them – the twins clamouring for his attention, Ruby jumping up and down, and Mum beaming.

Dad, his face glowing with pride, held out his hand. "Well done, Sidney," he said. His rough, calloused hand grabbed Sid's. "I'm proud to shake your hand. I'm that proud of you, son. I couldn't be more proud."

Sid found himself grinning from ear to ear, the pain of loss disappearing under the boisterous tide of his family's enthusiasm. "Thanks, Dad," he said, shaking his father's hand enthusiastically and trying not to wince at his dad's firm grip.

"We're going to collect our winnings," said Mum. She looked around. "Where's Auntie Glad?"

The family stopped talking and everyone stared around in dismay.

"She was with us a minute ago," said Mum. "We'll never find her in this crowd."

A slender figure stepped out from the crowd, leading a little old lady by the hand. It was Kiri, the tea towel wrapping her arm replaced by a sling, neatly folded and pinned. "I found this lady wandering around by herself," she said. "She told me she was looking for Sidney Everett."

Auntie Glad marched up to Sid. "They left me behind," she said. "What a bunch!" She glared at Dad, then looked Sid up and down.

"Look at you," she said. "Every inch a hero. A winner, if there ever was one."

Sid laughed. "Thanks, Auntie Glad," he said, allowing himself to be kissed on the cheek.

His eyes met Kiri's. "Thank you," he said.

"No worries. You rescued me. Now I rescued your auntie. We're even." She laughed. "Just joking."

Sid's heart missed a beat. How had he been so stupid? Hanging onto a hope about Sarah, when he'd known in his heart that the school-days relationship was gone. And all the time, here was Kiri, the best of the best.

"It was nothing," he muttered, hoping to shut her up before his family wanted to know the whole story.

But it was too late. Mum was already raising an inquisitive eyebrow. "What's this all about, Sidney?" she asked.

"Oh, nothing Mum." Sid squirmed.

"He just rescued me from a deep hole in the ground, that's all. Helped my uncle to safety, that's all. Nothing much," said Kiri.

"That sounds exciting, Sidney," said Mum. "You'll have to tell us all about it."

"Not now, Mum," muttered Sid.

"Later," she said.

"Yes, later," said Sid. "Mum? This is Kiri, from Ridgeways."

"Pleased to meet you, Kiri," said Mum.

"Pleased to meet you, too," said Kiri.

"Come on, you lot. Let's get our winnings," said Dad. "Then let's go home and celebrate."

"I'll catch you up," said Sid.

"What?" said Dad. "Don't you want to see how much money we get?"

Sid laughed. "You can show it to me later. I just want to…"

Beryl understood. She'd been watching Kiri and Sid. "He's got things he needs to sort out. Haven't you, Sid?" Her eyes sparkled.

"Um…" Sid looked at Kiri, then back at Beryl. "Yup. I have. I won't be long."

He turned back to Kiri. Her eyes met his, glowing with warmth and good humour. Teasing eyes, but kind eyes. The eyes of someone he knew he could trust. And he'd been fighting with himself about his feelings for her for quite long enough.

His little sister Ruby threw her arms around him. He rumpled her curls and squatted down to be eye to eye with her. "This is Kiri, Ruby," he said. "She's my friend."

"Hello," said Ruby. She took hold of Sid's hand. "I like your friend," she said.

"That's good," said Sid.

"Are you coming home?" Ruby asked.

"Soon," he said. "You go with Mum. I want to talk to Kiri."

Ruby glanced up at Kiri and nodded her head. "Okay," she said. She skipped away to where Mum was waiting for her.

Sid hardly noticed as his family disappeared into the crowd.

Chapter Forty

Christchurch Square

Sid stood with his family in Christchurch Square, surrounded by bustling throngs of Christmas shoppers. A hubbub of conversation and laughter filled the air, combined with the sharp tapping of heels on the hard pavement. In the centre of the square, a giant Christmas tree blazed with coloured electric lights. Behind it, the towering cathedral glowed golden in the evening sunlight.

The Salvation Army band that had been playing Christmas carols next to the tree, had stopped for a break before the next round of hymns.

Sid raised his eyes to the deepening blue of the sky above, filled with long streamers of gold and crimson cloud trailing towards the sunset. Pigeons cooed and squabbled as they fluttered and swooped through the warm summer air, looking for places to roost for the coming night. The last rays of sunlight gilded the high spire of the cathedral and glanced off the pigeons' whirring wings.

Sid looked at his parents. Mum and Dad were gazing around like kids at a fairground. Mum's eyes were sparkling. "I do love Christmas," she said. "It's a tremendous fuss, but it's so nice all the same."

Dad rolled his eyes. "You say that every year," he said.

The twins were searching through their pockets for coins. They hadn't quite done all of their Christmas shopping, and there was a shortfall. They went to Mum for help.

Beryl approached across the square, coming from the direction of Deaconess House, where she was a boarder. She was wearing a flowery summer frock and a short-sleeved knitted cardigan. Her high heels clicked smartly as she approached.

She looks very grown up, Sid thought.

Ruby waved to some children across the square.

Sid tapped her shoulder. "Who are they, Ruby?" he asked.

"My friends from school," she said. Her words were clear and easy to understand. He was impressed.

Kids from the deaf school, he thought. She has friends now.

Kiri stood next to him, so close he could easily have taken her hand, but he didn't quite dare to.

Beryl joined the family group, beaming, and grabbed Sid into a hug. "Good to see you, little brother," she said. She grinned, hesitating, then punched him on the arm.

"Ouch!" said Sid.

She punched him again. "Two for luck," she said. She lifted her chin, as if daring him to punch her back, then she winked at Kiri. "Hello," she said. Her eyes twinkled. "Lovely to see you again."

The deaf children across the square were signing something to Ruby, and she signed back immediately. Fluid, energetic signing, communicating effortlessly over the heads of the noisy crowd.

"They're not supposed to sign," Beryl said to Kiri. "They're supposed to learn to talk. But look at them! They always find a way."

Sid tapped Ruby on the shoulder again. "What are they saying, Rubes?" he asked.

"They ask who you are. I say you're my brother." She turned back to look at her friends, signing again, across the square.

"What are they saying now?" asked Sid.

"Merry Christmas," she said. This time, her words weren't quite perfect, but they were perfectly clear to Sid. She beamed and said it again. "Merry Christmas!"

Amazing, Sid thought, how they can talk to each other across a crowded space without having to shout. And nobody can understand it, except them. It's like a secret code.

"Merry Christmas, Ruby," he answered, his heart flooding with an overwhelming sense of gratitude. He felt like time and place had just that minute clicked together in a special way. A precious moment, never experienced before.

Unique, he thought. Like the perfect happy ending to a good book. Maybe life was like that. Now and then, you experienced a unique moment.

The Salvation Army band began to play 'God Rest Ye, Merry Gentlemen'. Sid's hand found Kiri's. Her fingers twined with his, and she leaned in closer to him.

"Merry Christmas, Sid," she whispered.

He smiled and leaned his head closer to hers. "Merry Christmas, Kiri," he said.

Author's Note

Thank you for reading *Like The Wind!*

If you would like to leave a review, I would greatly appreciate it! Please leave your review on whichever platform you prefer to use for reading or for giving reviews, or contact me directly via my website, https://jlwilliamsauthor.com

The characters in this book, and the horses, are entirely fictitious, except for Bill Broughton who was a famous New Zealand jockey in the 1940s. Christchurch is a real place, and the New Zealand Cup is a real race. The winner of the New Zealand Cup Race in 1947, the year in which this book is set, was not Manawa, it was a horse named Beau Le Harve.

Post-War trauma wasn't known at PTSD in the 1940s as it is today. It wasn't well understood, but was widely suffered, both by those returning from war and those who had been held in prisoner of war camps, as in this book.

If you would like to know when my next book, *Dark Island*, will be available, please visit my website, https://jlwilliamsauthor.com and join my email list or contact me directly. *Dark Island* is the first book in a historical mystery series set in New Zealand in 1901.

About the Author

J L Williams writes fast paced books about young people who follow their dreams. J L Williams lives in the north of New Zealand. She likes sunny mornings, stormy nights, and holidays by the sea. Her favourite books are mysteries.

9 781738 595136